Allison smiled malevolently.

"I haven't met a girl at a pageant yet who didn't have a skeleton in her closet. I intend to find out yours."

Nothing showed on Willow's beautiful face as she replied, "I have nothing to hide."

"Oh, really?" Allison asked coolly. "Well, we'll see about that, Miss Perfect." Her eyes narrowed to angry, cold slits. "Katie-the-cow isn't really worth my time. I think I'm going to ruin you, instead. And there's not a thing in the world that you can do about it."

Pageant

THE SOUTHERN GIRLS

CHERIE BENNETT

BERKLEY JAM BOOKS, NEW YORK

PAGEANT: THE SOUTHERN GIRLS

A Berkley Jam Book / published by arrangement with
the author

PRINTING HISTORY
Berkley Jam edition / June 1998

The Penguin Putnam Inc. World Wide Web site address is
http://www.penguinputnam.com

ISBN: 0-425-16377-6

BERKLEY JAM BOOKS®
Berkley Jam Books are published by The Berkley Publishing Group,
a member of Penguin Putnam Inc.,
200 Madison Avenue, New York, New York 10016.
BERKLEY JAM and its logo are trademarks
belonging to Berkley Publishing Corporation.

PRINTED IN THE UNITED STATES OF AMERICA

10 9 8 7 6 5 4 3 2 1

The PAGEANT series is dedicated to every
young woman with a dream, who is willing to work
hard enough to make her dream come true

"Some people look at things that are and ask why.
I dream things that never were and ask, why not?"

—BOBBY KENNEDY

CHAPTER
1

"I must be out of my mind," Katie Laramie told Jane Emery as she gazed nervously around the crowded ballroom of the Regency Hotel. "I don't belong at a beauty pageant!"

Jane looked pointedly at the large banner on the far wall of the ballroom that read WELCOME MISS TEEN SPIRIT SOUTHERN REGIONAL PAGEANT, then she turned her eyes to the white satin ribbon Katie wore diagonally across her chest that read MISS TEEN SPIRIT VIRGINIA. "It sure looks to me like you belong here, Miss Teen Spirit Virginia."

"Well, the judges in Virginia must have had a case of temporary insanity or something," Katie said. "I am *not* a beauty queen! Jane, I have thunder thighs!"

"As I have told you ten thousand times, the Miss Teen Spirit Pageant is about a lot more than beauty," Jane said patiently. "And you don't have thunder thighs."

"Compared to her I do," Katie observed as a tall, willowy, stunningly beautiful girl with long, white-blond hair floated by. Her banner read MISS TEEN SPIRIT LOUISIANA. "With my luck, she'll probably be my roommate."

Katie's heart hammered in her chest as her eyes scanned the ballroom again. There were parents, friends, pageant officials, as well as dozens of gorgeous girls wearing banners proclaiming their titles. To nervous Katie, they all seemed prettier, thinner, and infinitely more self-assured than she was.

"Hey, come on," Jane coaxed, hugging Katie's shoulders. "You're supposed to be enjoying this!"

Jane Emery, in her early twenties, was Katie's guidance counselor at Bayside High School in Back Bay, Virginia. But in the past three years she and Katie had become such close friends that Jane was really more like a big sister.

It was Jane who had showed Katie the article in *Teen Spirit* magazine about the very first Miss Teen Spirit Pageant. And it was Jane who had talked her into entering.

At first, Katie had just laughed at the idea. For one thing, she was five feet five inches tall, and weighed a hundred and thirty pounds—not exactly svelte beauty-pageant material. And although she had nice, shiny brown hair and reasonably nice big brown eyes, in her mind that added up to only okay looking. And okay-looking girls didn't win beauty pageants.

For another thing, Katie had no talent, unless you counted teaching her dog, Fleatrap, to roll over and play dead, or the weenie flips she could do on a trampoline.

No beauty. No talent.

Not entering, Katie told Jane.

Local winner gets two thousand dollars. Regional winners get five thousand dollars. Miss Teen Spirit gets ten thousand dollars, a new car, a new wardrobe, and *a four year all-expenses-paid scholarship to any college of her choice that accepts her as a student,* Jane told Katie.

Wow.

Katie's dream was to go to Harvard. And her family was, frankly . . . poor.

Imagine, a four-year scholarship to Harvard.

Not that she'd ever actually win, of course, but . . .

She let Jane talk her into entering.

And to her great shock, she had won the state pageant. Now here she was, at the opening tea for the Southern Regional Pageant, overcome with fear, insecurity, and anxiety. The good news was that as Miss Teen Spirit Virginia, she was two thousand dollars richer, less what she had spent on clothes for this pageant. The bad news was, she felt like a big, fat, stupid fraud.

"Hey, I need to find the ladies' room," Jane said. "I think it's out in the lobby."

"I'll come with you," Katie offered quickly.

"You will not," Jane declared. "You'll stay here and mingle like you're supposed to. Besides, the orientation is going to start soon, and it's a long drive back home."

Katie grabbed her sleeve. "You're deserting me?"

"Katie Laramie, you have everything it takes to win," Jane told her firmly. "You just remember that."

"I'll try," Katie said. "Thank you. For everything. If it wasn't for you . . ."

"I'm so proud of you." Jane hugged her tight and hurried away so Katie wouldn't see the tears in her eyes.

Now that she was all alone, Katie felt even more self-conscious than she had before.

Okay, Katie, she told herself. *Just go up to someone, anyone, and introduce yourself. You can do it.*

"Oh, wow, you're Miss Teen Spirit Virginia!" a petite, darling, African-American girl exclaimed as she scurried over to Katie. "Cool! I'm Gigi Gerrard, Miss Teen Spirit Southern Dove—like the banner says. What a zoo in here, huh?"

"I'm Katie Laramie." She gratefully shook Gigi's out-stretched hand. "It *is* kind of overwhelming."

"Oh, it doesn't bother me," Gigi proclaimed airily. "I sing in front of huge crowds at these gospel conventions. So, what's your talent?"

"In my case, you mean lack of talent," Katie said ruefully. "I can't sing or dance or—"

"So how'd you win Miss Virginia?"

"I did tricks on a trampoline," she admitted meekly.

"Well, I guess your tricks must be really good!" Gigi laughed.

Katie laughed, too. "Trust me, they're not. I love your skirt, by the way," she added.

Gigi had on a long, stretchy skirt printed with huge red poppies on a black background. Over that she wore a pretty, fitted, red crocheted short-sleeved sweater.

Katie was kind of surprised. Most of the girls in the room were conservatively dressed, because they thought it would help their chances. The room abounded with pretty girls in slightly fitted pastel-colored suits, with the skirt ending just above the knee.

In fact, Katie, who usually lived in jeans (she wasn't all that into clothes, and she could rarely afford to buy any, anyway) had used some of her precious two-thousand-dollar winnings to buy a conservative-but-cute wardrobe for the regional pageant, as suggested in the pageant manual of helpful tips. At the moment she had on a light blue sheath dress with a matching light blue jacket. It was unlike anything she had ever worn in her life.

"Your outfit is cute, too," Gigi told Katie.

Katie made a face. "It is not. I look like just about every other girl in here, and we all look like little pastel cookie cutters."

Gigi laughed. "Well, now that you mention it . . ."

"Believe me, the real me lives in ratty jeans and a

T-shirt," Katie said with a sigh. She looked at Gigi's banner. "What's Miss Southern Dove?"

"The Doves is a national organization for teens that promotes the values of Dr. Martin Luther King, Jr.," Gigi explained proudly.

"That sounds great."

"Yeah, it's fun," Gigi said. "It kinda saved my life, too. My dad is a minister, and my parents are so strict that if it were up to them, I wouldn't date until I was thirty. But they let me join the Doves, and that's where I met my boyfriend, Trey. He's a musician—totally to die for. Of course, my parents would kill me if they knew. They think Trey and I are just 'friends.'"

"Your secret is safe with me."

"Thanks." Gigi looked around the room. "Not a lot of girls with my complexion here, huh?" Her eyes lit on a girl in a wheelchair who had just entered the room. The girl stopped her wheelchair just inside the huge open doors to the ballroom.

"Look at that girl over there in the wheelchair," Gigi said.

"She's wearing a banner," Katie noticed. "I guess she's in the pageant."

"Maybe she broke her leg or something between her local pageant and this one," Gigi guessed. "Hey, it looks like she's all by herself. Let's go meet her!"

Enthusiastic Gigi half dragged Katie across the huge ballroom toward the girl in the wheelchair, confidently weaving her way through the crowd.

"Hi, I'm Gigi, this is Katie," Gigi announced when they'd reached the girl.

She looked up at them. Her banner read MISS TEEN SPIRIT MISSISSIPPI. She was very pretty, with chestnut curls and huge blue eyes, and she wore a cute outfit: a pink-and-yellow polka-dot minidress with yellow-and-pink-striped tights underneath. On her head she wore a pink beret with yellow daisies on it. She wasn't smiling.

"I'm Dawn Faison," the girl said.

"Nice to meet you," Gigi said. "So, did you break your leg or something?"

"Do you see a cast on my leg?" Dawn asked.

"Well, no," Gigi admitted. "But I had this friend who broke her leg and they didn't even put it in a cast because—"

"I didn't break my leg," Dawn said. "I'm a paraplegic. Meaning I'm paralyzed from the waist down."

Gigi put her hand over her eyes and made a face. "Well, I'm a major idiot. I open my mouth, I insert my foot. My boyfriend says that all the time." She peeked out from between her fingers. "I'm really sorry."

"Forget it," Dawn said, and she smiled for the first time. "Believe me, I know that no one expects a girl stuck in a wheelchair to be wearing one of these banners. Frankly, no one was as shocked to win this thing as I was."

"Oh, I was pretty shocked to win my pageant, too," Katie said. "I mean, I never thought that—"

"Hey, y'all, I hope I'm not interrupting," a pretty blond-haired girl with a thick Southern accent said, walking over to them. Her banner read MISS TEEN SPIRIT PRIDE OF THE SOUTH. She was wearing a pink outfit very similar to Katie's. "I just thought I'd try and introduce myself to as many people as possible. I'm Scarlett-Caress Latham."

The other girls all introduced themselves to Scarlett.

"It's Scarlett-Caress," she corrected them sweetly. "You know, a hyphenate."

"Oh, we see," Dawn said solemnly.

"I'm just so proud to be here, aren't you?" Scarlett-Caress gushed.

"I think it's gonna be a blast," Gigi said. "Have you been in any pageants before?"

"Oh, tons." Scarlett-Caress smiled. "They're really super. I always meet the sweetest girls at pageants." Her eyes lit on Dawn. "I think it's just wonderful that you're here."

"Why?" Dawn asked.

"Well, you know, I believe that girls of all races, creeds, colors, and infirmities are equal," Scarlett-Caress said.

"That's very deep," Dawn agreed, feigning sincerity.

"Thank you. Well, it was nice to have met y'all. See y'all later!" Scarlett-Caress walked on to introduce herself to another nearby group of girls.

"How fake can you get?" Dawn asked. "That girl is so sweet she could give you diabetes!"

"Her name sounds like a disease." Gigi giggled, then dramatically clutched at her throat. "Save me, Doctor! I've come down with the dreaded Scarlett-Caress disease from overdosing on too much sugar!"

"I wonder what Miss Pride of the South is," Katie mused.

"If you read through everything in that huge pageant handbook—which I didn't, but my mother did," Gigi added, "it explains that national organizations who qualify can hold local contests, and the girl who wins can compete regionally."

"Like you with the Doves, " Katie said, nodding.

"Right. I know there's a Miss Northern Dove competing in the Northeast Regional Pageant in New York," Gigi said. "So maybe there's a Miss Pride of the North, too."

"But I'll bet she isn't as 'super' as Scarlett-Caress," Dawn said sarcastically. "Even though I'm stuck in a wheelchair, she believes I'm almost human. I, for one, am deeply touched."

"Does it bother you when people say something dumb like she did?" Katie asked Dawn.

"Please," Dawn scoffed. "That girl is like some kind of beauty-pageant windup doll. I mean, you can't take her seriously!"

"She'll probably win," Katie said with a sigh.

The other two girls looked after Scarlett and sighed, too. She was *exactly* the kind of girl who came to mind when they pictured the winner of a big beauty pageant.

"We just have to remember that Miss Teen Spirit isn't some shallow beauty pageant," Katie said, repeating exactly what Jane had told her over and over. "If it was, I wouldn't be here."

"Me, either." Gigi lifted the bottom of her sweater and flashed a small silver navel ring. "There's got to be some beauty-pageant law against this!"

"I thought your parents were so conservative," Katie said, laughing.

"They are. I just never let them see my navel." Gigi shrugged, then glanced over again at Scarlett-Caress, who was laughing with Miss Tennessee. "Look at it this way. Granted, Miss Scarlett over there has got that beauty-pageant thing going on, but the three of us won just like she did. Which means any of us could win the whole enchilada!"

"You know," Dawn said, "I like you. I mean, you're delusional, but I like you."

"Look, whatever happens, let's have fun," Katie decided.

"And we'll hang out together," Gigi added.

"Deal," Dawn said.

"Deal," Katie agreed, relieved to have made two friends. She felt better already. After all, she'd never expected to meet two girls she really liked so quickly. They weren't anything at all like the kind of girls she had expected to meet at the pageant. She truly felt as if they wouldn't get all weird if she told them how poor her family was.

Like so poor that they had once been on welfare and food stamps.

Like so poor they sometimes ate noodles with ketchup for dinner, and were happy to get it.

Her little brother gathered empty soda cans from trash bins so he could collect the refund money.

The church charity ladies brought them a turkey for Thanksgiving.

Like *so* poor that Harvard was just some sort of faraway dream that could never really happen to a girl like her.

Unless she won Miss Teen Spirit.

Unless she really won.

CHAPTER

2

" *L* adies and gentlemen, if I might have your attention," a cultured female voice called through the sound system.

The room grew quiet as everyone turned their eyes toward a beautiful, perfectly groomed woman who was standing on the small stage that had been erected under the welcoming banner. In folding chairs to her right sat four women and four men, their expressions unreadable.

"At this time I'd like to ask family and guests if they would excuse themselves from the ballroom." The woman spoke smoothly into the microphone. "We promise to take good care of your girls. Remember, they're *our* girls, too!"

Guests or family who had accompanied a contestant to Nashville said their sometimes tearful good-byes, until finally only the contestants and pageant officials were left in the ballroom.

"Now, girls, if you would all have seats here." With a nod of her head, the woman indicated the rows of folding chairs that had been assembled in front of the stage.

The air was charged with excitement as the contestants

found seats. Katie and Gigi picked chairs at the end of a row so they could sit with Dawn, who made a joke about always bringing her own chair.

"For those of you who don't know me, I'm Mrs. Elizabeth Crownwell-Stevens, the national coordinator for the Miss Teen Spirit Pageant," the woman at the microphone announced.

The girls applauded dutifully.

"Thank you." Mrs. Crownwell-Stevens acknowledged their welcome. "It is my great pleasure to welcome you girls to the Miss Teen Spirit Southern Regional Pageant. During the next two weeks, you thirty girls will share the experience of a lifetime, culminating in our Southern Regional Pageant. As you know, only six of you will be chosen to go on to the nationally televised Miss Teen Spirit Pageant. But please believe me when I tell you that all thirty of you are winners in our eyes."

The girls applauded again.

"Under your seats, you'll each find your orientation folder," Mrs. Crownwell-Stevens continued.

There was a rustle as all the girls retrieved their folders, each embossed with the raised gold Miss Teen Spirit logo.

"You'll find a list of all of your room assignments here at the hotel," Mrs. Crownwell-Stevens went on, "as well as the name of your roommate. After we finish our orientation, you are all free to go to your rooms to freshen up for tonight's dinner with the judges and meet your roommate. You'll find that your luggage has already been delivered."

Katie was dazzled. The truth was, she had only ever stayed in a motel, and certainly never a grand hotel like this one. And since she didn't own any luggage (all she had was an ancient backpack she used for camping), she had borrowed Jane's for the pageant.

She scanned the list of names to find her roommate—someone named Willow Rose Harrison.

Too bad I didn't luck out and get Gigi or Dawn, Katie thought.

"Someone please tell me this is some kind of cosmic joke." Dawn was staring at the roommate list and shaking her head.

Gigi hurried over to her. "Why, who'd you get?"

Dawn rolled her eyes. "There is only one Scarlett-Caress here, I assume."

"*She's* your roommate?" Katie asked.

"Lucky me."

"Has anyone met someone named Beth Kaplan?" Gigi asked.

Dawn and Katie both shook their heads no.

"Well, she's my roomie," Gigi told them.

"Maybe we could put her and Miss Scarlett together," Dawn suggested hopefully.

"We're all supposed to love each other way too much to want to change roommates," Gigi pointed out.

"Before we continue, I'd like to ask our six wonderful judges to stand." Onstage, Mrs. Crownwell-Stevens was again speaking.

Six of the eight people seated on the stage stood up as the girls applauded again.

"Your judges will be wearing their official blue ribbons at all times during the next two weeks, so you'll always be able to recognize them," Mrs. Crownwell-Stevens said. "And just a little tip, girls. Not recognizing a judge even *without* a ribbon isn't a very good idea."

There was a chuckle from the contestants.

The judges sat down. "I'd also like you to meet Broadway choreographer Jimmy Delancy, who will be putting you girls through your paces in all the dance numbers."

A tall thin guy with a buzz cut stood up, waved at the girls, and sat back down.

"All right, girls, let's go over your schedule. It's printed on the blue sheets in your folder. The first week will be a whirlwind of Nashville fun—Opryland Hotel, the Wild Horse Saloon, et cetera—they're all specifically listed for you.

"Remember, girls, that the judges will always be at the events, and you are being judged at all times. You'll also have time to work on your talent, and Jimmy will begin teaching you your choreography for the group numbers. You'll also have extensive preliminary private interviews with the judges, and each of you will have the opportunity to speak in public on your chosen platform subject."

The girls all knew that their platform subject meant the subject they had chosen to concentrate on for their community service. Their community-service and platform speeches counted for a quarter of their final points.

"What's your platform?" Gigi whispered to Katie.

"Teens Against Drunk Driving," Katie whispered back. "What's yours?"

"Music Therapy for Underprivileged Kids," Gigi replied. "How about you, Dawn?"

"Belly Dancing for Paraplegics," Dawn replied, straight-faced.

Katie and Gigi started to crack up but got themselves back under control as Mrs. Crownwell-Stevens again spoke up.

"The second week, things will really heat up. As you'll see on your schedule, you'll be busy from morning to night with talent rehearsals, dinners, choreography rehearsals, and preliminary judging.

"Girls, I'm sure by now you're well aware of how seriously we take the moral tone of our pageant. All of you are between your junior and senior years of high school right now. All of you, by the rules of this pageant, are under eighteen. As such, we are totally responsible for you at all times.

"A chaperon has been assigned to each set of roommates. She will stay in the room directly next door to your room. There will be bed check every night, and you are never—let me repeat, *never,* allowed to be with anyone or do anything that has not been cleared with your chaperon first. To do so can and will lead to immediate dismissal from the pageant."

Now Mrs. Crownwell-Stevens smiled at them. "There's a list of all the obvious rules—no smoking, no drinking, et cetera—but I don't think I need to belabor the point. And now I'd like to allow all of you to find your rooms and rest up for our dinner this evening, where you will have a chance to meet and mingle with your judges.

"We hope that this experience enriches your lives. You are all very, very special young women. Thank you."

The girls applauded enthusiastically. Scarlett-Caress jumped to her feet, and instantly other girls, sorry they hadn't thought of it first, joined her.

"Well, I guess we go find our rooms." Katie was starting to feel nervous all over again.

"And our roomies," Dawn added glumly.

"Dawn!" Scarlett-Caress cried, running over to her. "We're roomies! Isn't that so fantastic?"

"I was just marveling at it myself," Dawn said.

"Want me to wheel you?" Scarlett-Caress asked.

"The chair has a motor," Dawn pointed out.

"Wow, isn't that clever?" Scarlett-Caress opened her eyes in an expression resembling surprise. "So, let's go, roomie!"

Dawn shot Gigi and Katie a look, then she wheeled off with Scarlett-Caress.

"That is not what I would call a good match," Katie remarked as they headed for the lobby.

"No kidding," Gigi agreed. At a special lobby desk set up for the contestants, they got their room keys, then headed for the bank of elevators. A well-dressed couple walked by and, noticing their pageant ribbons, wished them luck. A cute young guy in a cowboy hat winked at them.

"This attention is fun!" Gigi winked back at the cute guy.

"I don't think you're supposed to do that," Katie said nervously. "There's got to be a no-flirting rule, or something."

"I live, therefore I flirt—that's my motto," Gigi told her. They wedged themselves into an elevator stuffed with other girls, half of whom got off with them on the tenth floor.

"Here's my room." Gigi stopped in front of a door marked 1055. "Want me to knock on your door and we can go down to the reception together later?"

"That would be great," Katie replied. "I guess my room is around the corner."

Katie left Gigi and found her room a moment later; she turned the key in the lock, and opened the door. She felt really nervous—it would be the first time in her life she'd be sharing a room with a total stranger.

The room was empty.

On one side was Katie's single shabby suitcase. On the other side were eight pieces of expensive matching luggage.

Willow Rose Harrison is rich, Katie thought, feeling even more insecure. *Just my luck.*

She thought she heard a noise coming from the bathroom and knocked on the bathroom door.

"Hello?"

No answer, but more muffled sounds.

"I won't disturb you," Katie said quickly. "I'm your roommate, Katie. And I just wanted to let you know I'm here."

As Katie was walking away from the bathroom she heard

a loud crash from inside. She rushed back to the door. "Are you okay?" she called through the door. "Did you hurt yourself?"

A loud groan.

"Willow?"

Katie didn't know what to do. What if her roommate was in there dying or something? On the other hand, maybe she just had bad cramps, and she certainly wouldn't want some total stranger bothering her.

"If you just answer me, I'll know you're okay and I'll leave you alone," Katie called out.

No answer, just another groan.

Without hesitating another moment, Katie reached out and turned the doorknob. To her surprise it wasn't locked.

Sitting there on the floor of the bathroom was the tall, spectacularly gorgeous girl with the white-blond hair that Katie had seen when she and Jane had first entered the ballroom.

But now, instead of looking like perfection, Willow's hair was a mess and her makeup was blotched all over her face. She looked awful.

"Willow? Are you okay?" Katie asked.

"I'm sick," Willow managed, her voice slurred. "I fell."

"Let me help you." Katie reached out for the other girl. "Do you need a doctor?"

"No!" Willow said quickly. "It's just a flu thing. Can you help me up?"

Katie managed to heave her from the bathroom floor and half carried her to one of the beds. While she was doing so her face came very close to the other girl's, and suddenly Katie's head jerked back.

Willow reeked of alcohol.

She wasn't sick at all.

Willow Rose Harrison was dead-drunk.

CHAPTER

G igi was hanging up the last of her clothes when she heard the door open. She turned around. At the doorway stood a pretty, slender girl with long, straight brown hair.

"Beth?" Gigi asked.

The girl nodded. "Beth Kaplan," she said, shaking Gigi's hand. "I was downstairs making a long-distance call to my violin teacher on the pay phone, and it took forever."

"I'm Gigi Gerrard. So you play the violin, huh?"

Beth nodded, went to her suitcase, and began to unpack. "I've been studying since I was four. I'm hoping to go to Berklee College of Music in Boston to study classical violin." She hung some dresses in their closet.

"You mean you're hoping to win a scholarship to Berklee, compliments of this pageant." Gigi bounced up and down on her bed as she spoke.

"I admit, I *am* hopeful," Beth said seriously. She carried some toiletries into the bathroom.

"Judges love that classical-music stuff," Gigi called to her.

"That's somewhat true," Beth said, coming out of the bathroom. "I charted the winners and runners-up of various national pageants that have a talent division, and only vocalists of popular songs have won more often than classical musicians."

"You actually *charted* this?"

Beth nodded, and put her neat piles of underwear in the dresser drawers. "I try to do things thoroughly. Of course, I couldn't chart Miss Teen Spirit, because this is the first pageant."

"Uh-huh." Amazed, Gigi stifled a laugh.

This Beth girl really needs to lighten up, she thought. *She's the most serious girl I ever met. Talk about a mismatch of roommates!*

"There's something I'd like to get out of the way," Beth began, sitting on her bed. "Would you prefer that I refer to you as black or African-American?"

This time Gigi couldn't help herself; she really did laugh. "Would you prefer that I refer to you as Caucasian or white?"

"Either would be fine," Beth replied, nodding.

"Hey, I'm teasing you." Gigi jumped up from her bed. "All you have to do is call me Gigi, okay? Black, African-American, whatever floats your boat. It's not like either one is a racial slur, ya know?"

"I just wanted to make you feel comfortable."

Gigi padded over to the closet and got her robe. "Beth, do you know anyone black?"

"Not really," Beth admitted. "There are a couple of black girls in my high-school class in Florida, but it's a huge school, and I don't really know them."

"Well, I've got black friends and I've got white friends and none of them are any better or worse because of the color of their skin, so, really, you can chill out."

"I'll try to do that." Beth nodded again. "I hope you'll help me. I feel that I could learn a lot from this experience."

Gigi laughed. "Hey, Beth, did anyone ever mention that you're awfully *serious*?"

"Yes." Beth sighed. "I get told that all the time. My own parents tell me that."

Gigi leaned over and patted her roommate on the head. "They're right. So try and just chill, okay? Because serious is about the last thing anyone ever called *this* party girl."

"You're serious about wanting to win the pageant, though, aren't you?"

"As a heart attack." Gigi lifted her sweater over her head and threw the garment on her bed. "I'm in the shower."

At that moment the phone rang. Beth leaned over and picked it up. "Hello?"

"Hi, is Gigi Gerrard there, please?" came a deep, male voice.

"One moment, please," Beth said into the phone. She held it out to Gigi, her hand covering the voice piece. "It's for you. Male."

"Young and sexy, as in my boyfriend, or middle-aged Baptist preacher, as in my daddy?"

"I'd say young and sexy," Beth decided.

Gigi grinned and bounced over to the bed in two giant leaps, grabbing the phone from Beth. "Trey, baby?"

"Did you win yet?" Trey teased.

"Oh, Trey." Gigi sighed, falling back on her bed. "I miss you so much."

"I miss you, too. How's it going?" he asked.

"Well, my roommate is this totally wild woman with three tattoos on her butt," Gigi said wickedly. She sat up in time to watch Beth's jaw drop open and her face turn red.

"I'm teasing," Gigi assured Trey and Beth at the same time. "She's really nice. Her name's Beth. And I met these other great girls, already. Katie and Dawn."

"Are there any other sisters in the competition?" Trey asked.

"I saw one," Gigi said. "I didn't get to talk to her yet."

"Two black girls out of—what did you tell me?—thirty girls?" Trey asked skeptically. "You think a black girl can really win?"

"Don't go making this a racial thing, Trey," Gigi protested. "Tell me more about how much you miss me instead."

"I'd like to be there to show you how much I miss you," Trey murmured softly.

Gigi felt sexy, little thrills in her stomach just thinking about Trey's kisses. *I love him so much*, she thought.

She closed her eyes and pictured him in her mind. *Six feet tall, smooth brown skin, strong arms, the most beautiful eyes in the world. And his lips* . . .

"Gigi? You lost in thought again?" Trey asked.

"I was thinking that I wish I could tell my parents about us." Gigi wasn't about to tell him that she was dreaming about his kisses. It might go to his head.

"We won't have to sneak around forever," Trey promised her. "Once you're eighteen—"

"Trey, I just turned seventeen a month ago! I'll die if I have to wait a whole year. Besides, there is no guarantee in this world that my parents will let me see you even after I turn eighteen."

"I don't know what your daddy's problem is, Gigi. It's not like I'm a gangsta rapper or something."

"According to my father, if it isn't gospel or classical, it isn't music. Plus, you're nineteen and you dropped out of college. He won't need to hear anything else."

"Well, baby, it's not your daddy I'm in love with, now, is it? Want me to call you tomorrow?"

"You know I do," Gigi answered.

"Count on it," Trey said. "We get into Detroit about three. I'll call you from there. And Gigi?"

"What?"

"I'm planning to dream X-rated dreams tonight. Starring you. Bye, baby."

"Bye." Slowly she hung up the phone. "I miss him so much."

"I heard you say he's a musician," Beth said.

Gigi nodded. "Keyboards. He got hired to tour with Mason Belmont, and he dropped out of college so he could go. He's been on the road for six months already."

"Mason Belmont. He's a jazz composer who plays saxophone, right?"

"Good for you, Beth," Gigi teased.

"I happen to like some jazz," Beth said.

Gigi got up and headed for the bathroom again. "Next week Mason's band is playing a club in Memphis. That's not far from Nashville."

"No, it isn't."

Gigi leaned dreamily against the wall. "I can just picture it. Trey comes here to be with me. My parents are far away in Atlanta and we don't have to sneak around. . . ."

"But if you got caught with him here, you'd be disqualified from the pageant."

"Uh-huh. Well, that's a big ol' if, isn't it," Gigi said with bravado. "You know what I think?"

"What?" Beth asked.

"I think that sometimes you have to be willing to risk everything for true love."

"I just think it's amazing that you can dress yourself."
Scarlett-Caress marveled as Dawn slipped the pretty peach
linen dress she was wearing to the opening dinner over her
head.

*And I think it's amazing that you can speak in complete
sentences, you moron,* Dawn thought.

She didn't say it aloud, though. She and Scarlett-Caress
had been in their room for two hours now, and in that time
Dawn had found herself having to bite back sarcastic retorts
about once every five minutes. She had promised herself at
least to try to get along with Scarlett-Caress. After all,
they'd be spending two weeks sharing a hotel room.

Two *long* weeks.

"You know, it's truly an amazing coincidence that we're
roomies," Scarlett-Caress confessed. She was sitting at the
desk applying her makeup in front of a specially lit makeup
mirror she had brought with her. "Do you know what my
platform is?"

"Nope."

Scarlett-Caress spun around to face Dawn. "It's Special
Olympics. You know, Olympic sports for physically challenged people. They win ribbons and everything!"

"*Special* Olympics is for people with mental handicaps,"
Dawn said, her voice even. "*Wheelchair* Olympics is for
athletes in wheelchairs."

"Oh, I knew that," Scarlett-Caress said quickly. "But, you
know, some of the people in Special Olympics have
physical problems, too, bless their hearts. I just think the
world of them, really. You people are just so inspirational."
She turned back around and reached for her mascara.

Dawn could almost picture herself wringing Scarlett-

Caress's neck. But no. She wasn't going to let this girl get to her. She hadn't come all this way and worked this hard to lose it over an idiot like her roommate.

Fortunately, the pageant had made sure that she got a room specially designed for handicapped access, so Dawn was able to wheel herself into the bathroom through the extra-wide doorway. All she could see in the mirror was her head and the tops of her shoulders; if she wanted a better view of herself she'd have to stand up. But that was typical.

She reached for her water spritzer and sprayed her curls, then scrunched them with her favorite gel.

"Aren't you clever, spraying your curls like that," Scarlett-Caress observed from the doorway.

Dawn gritted her teeth and kept her mouth shut.

Scarlett leaned one slender hand on the door frame. "Dawn, if this is too painful for you to talk about, I will totally understand. But I was wondering how you ended up in your unfortunate condition."

"A swimming accident when I was thirteen," Dawn replied. This was a question she'd had to answer over and over during the Mississippi pageant. At first she'd hated answering. But now she was used to it. She brushed some pale pink blush across her cheeks.

"How utterly awful!" Scarlett-Caress cried. "You mean that until a few years ago you were normal?"

"If you mean could I walk and chew gum at the same time, the answer is yes. I was an athlete, actually. I won my first national juniors gold medal in swimming when I was eight."

"Oh, you poor, poor thing."

Dawn was shocked to see that there were tears in Scarlett-Caress's eyes.

Well, I don't like her any better for it, she thought. *Pity is the last thing I want from a bimbo like her.*

"Were you injured during a swim meet?" Scarlett-Caress asked.

"Nope." Dawn spoke to her own reflection in the mirror, and the memory came back to her as if it was only yesterday. "I was hanging out with my friends at the lake. We were all jumping off these rocks into the water. I jumped off a higher rock than anyone, except this one cute guy, Sean, who I really liked. Sean dared me to jump off an even higher rock. I really wanted him to like me, so . . ."

"So you jumped?" Scarlett-Caress asked, wide-eyed.

"I climbed up to the rock, and I was all ready to jump. But the rocks were wet, and my foot slipped. I fell."

Crack.

Dawn could still remember the exact sound of her back making sharp contact with the thick tree branch that had jutted out over the water.

Crack.

The sickening sound of her back breaking before she passed out.

Then she remembered nothing at all, except waking up in the hospital the next day, her parents' anxious faces looking down at her.

And how she couldn't feel her legs.

"Well, I just think you're the bravest thing," Scarlett-Caress gushed, rushing over to hug Dawn.

"It's not like I had a choice, Scarlett-Caress," Dawn pointed out. She wheeled herself out of the bathroom. Her roommate followed her.

"You know, I have a sensational idea," Scarlett-Caress said eagerly. She sat on her bed and leaned toward Dawn. "I've been in so many pageants, I know all the tricks of the trade. I'm talking about inside secrets you can only learn by experience."

"Go on," Dawn said cautiously.

"Well, Dawn, I'm going to share all my secrets with you," Scarlett-Caress said momentously. "Won't that be fun?"

Dawn cocked her head at her roommate. "Why would you do that?"

"To help you!"

"I repeat," Dawn said, "why would you do that?"

Scarlett-Caress reached for Dawn's hands and clutched them in her own. "Because, Dawn, you can inspire all the other poor little paralyzed girls out there. Why, with my help, you might even make the nationals! Wouldn't that be fantastic?"

If it wasn't so pathetic, it would be funny, Dawn realized. *Scarlett is willing—no, eager—to share pageant secrets with me, because she's absolutely certain that I could never win.*

She looked Scarlett earnestly in the eye. "Bless your heart, Scarlett-Caress."

"Oh, it's nothing," Scarlett-Caress insisted. "It's the least I can do. I mean—"

There was a knock on their door.

"Don't you move a muscle," Scarlett-Caress said, hurrying to the door.

She opened it. Standing there was a gorgeous girl with incredible red hair that hung in waves past her waist. She had on a short skirt covered in red sequins, topped by a blue-sequined vest. Her cowboy boots were red, white, and blue. In her hands was a white-sequined cowgirl hat.

"Hey, I'm Shyanne Derringer, from next door? I'm Miss Southern Rodeo Queen? I knocked and knocked on our chaperon's door, but she didn't answer. And I am just desperate for some Super Glue. I broke a nail."

"Gosh, sorry," Scarlett-Caress exclaimed. "I am totally out. I'm just sick that I can't help you."

"How about you?" Shyanne asked Dawn hopefully.

"Sorry." Dawn shook her head.

"Well, shoot." Shyanne sighed, "Thanks, anyway. I'll rustle some up, somewhere."

She headed down the hall to knock on the next door. Scarlett-Caress closed the door to their room and turned to Dawn. "Rule number one—never dress in a tacky outfit like she had on, except for when we parade in the costume of our choice to show state pride. Oh, and another thing. Your state pride costume should be cute but sexy. Not so sexy that they think you're slutty, though.

"Rule number two—always, always act like you want to help every girl in the pageant do her best." Scarlett-Caress walked over to her makeup bag and pulled out some Super Glue. She held it up. "But remember, the operative word in that sentence was '*act*.' She is the competition. She can find her own Super Glue."

Dawn was impressed in spite of herself. It was amazing. In the last two minutes she could have sworn that Scarlett-Caress's IQ had jumped thirty points.

Maybe she wasn't going to be such an awful roommate, after all.

CHAPTER

4

"You're sure you feel better?" Katie asked Willow doubtfully. "You still look really pale."

"That's just because I never go in the sun without wearing a total sunblock," Willow said. "Sun ages you faster than anything."

It was two hours later, and after drinking three cups of black coffee and taking a cold shower, Willow had managed to put on her hose and lingerie. Now she was standing at the bathroom mirror carefully applying her makeup.

Katie, who had already finished dressing, stood in the doorway to the bathroom. She had on a short-sleeved pale pink satin dress that ended just above her knee, and tiny rhinestone studs danced in her ears. She had found the dress on sale at the local mall. But even then the price tag had almost made her faint.

"Silly me, huh? Mixing allergy pills and cough medicine with alcohol in it?" Willow said, giving Katie a radiant smile.

Katie wanted to believe Willow, but she was doubtful.

After all, she had smelled Willow's breath, and she knew alcohol when she smelled it.

But I wc ·'t say anything, Katie decided. *Maybe she was just nervous about the orientation session and she had a couple of glasses of wine or something. Not that I can imagine a girl like Willow being nervous about anything. Or where she would have gotten the wine in the first place.*

"I guess you have to be careful, mixing medications like that," Katie said.

"From now on I absolutely will," Willow assured her as she gave her stunning white-blond hair a few extra strokes.

Katie watched the other girl brushing her hair, and her heart sank.

I bet that silk-and-lace teddy she's wearing cost more than my entire pageant wardrobe, she thought. *And on top of that, she looks totally perfect in it. I can't compete with perfect.*

Katie watched silently as Willow went to their closet and pulled out a dress, which she slipped over her head.

"Zip me," Willow asked, turning her back to Katie.

Katie obliged. When Willow turned around, Katie was awestruck. Her dress was a fluid column of white raw silk with a slightly scooped neckline that emphasized her long, graceful neck and bared her collarbones.

"That dress is gorgeous," Katie breathed.

"Thanks." Willow reached for a jewelry case on the dresser and took out some pearls. "Vera Wang designed it. Actually, she designed my entire pageant wardrobe."

"Isn't she the one who designed Nancy Kerrigan's skating outfits at the Olympics?"

Willow nodded and dropped the pearls around her neck. "It was my mother's idea. And it's so funny, because for the longest time she was totally against my being in this pageant. She's the state attorney general, and she was sure that all pageants were sexist and demeaning, and a total waste of my brains and abilities."

"Your mother is attorney general of the whole state of Louisiana?" Katie asked, awestruck.

Willow nodded. "And my father is chief public defender for New Orleans. They're both big shots in the Democratic party—sort of a Southern version of the Kennedy family . . . or so they like to think."

She smiled at Katie again. "Anyway, I had to literally prove to both of them that this isn't a beauty pageant, it's a *scholarship* pageant for girls. Once I won my dad over, he worked on my mom. And once my mom got won over, she decided to help me in her usual thorough fashion, meaning she went totally overboard."

"Like hiring Vera Wang," Katie said.

"And flying Céline Dion's vocal coach to New Orleans to work with me," Willow added. "My mother never does anything halfway. How about your parents?"

Well, let's see, Katie thought. *My dad is a Vietnam vet who was never the same mentally or physically after he came home from the war. He's on total disability and bounces in and out of mental hospitals. My mom works as a cashier at Revco. Her employee discount sure helps out when we can't afford toilet paper. . . .*

No. I could never, ever tell her or anyone else here the truth. No one would understand.

"My parents are fine," Katie said. "You know, small-town, sweet, regular."

"That sounds heavenly," Willow commented. "Sometimes I feel like I spend my life under a magnifying glass." She sprayed herself lightly with some French perfume. "Want some?"

"No, thanks," Katie said. She didn't want to admit that she had already sprayed herself with an inexpensive cologne her mother had brought home from the drugstore as a good-luck present.

As Willow put pearl studs into her ears she turned to Katie again. "Listen, can you do me two tiny favors?"

"Sure."

"Can you be an angel and go down the hall and get me some ice from the machine down there?" She reached for an ice bucket that was next to her jewelry case and tossed it to Katie. "I want to put some under my eyes. They're a little puffy still, don't you think?"

Katie didn't see anything puffy about Willow's eyes at all. In fact, she thought her roommate had the most beautiful violet-colored eyes she'd ever seen. Still, she was happy to help.

"No problem. What's the other favor?"

"I'll tell you when you get back," Willow promised, flashing her radiant smile again.

As soon as Katie was out the door, Willow hurried to the closet and got out a small suitcase she had stashed in the back. She took out a half-full bottle of vodka and drank three long gulps. Then she shuddered, the heat of the vodka hitting her.

Ahhhhh. I'm feeling better already, she thought as she leaned against the closet door. *People are so silly about drinking. It's not like I'm some kind of a lush. I just like the way it relaxes me.*

She cupped her hands to her mouth and blew. *Good thing vodka is odorless. But just in case . . .*

Willow hurried into the bathroom and gargled with some minty mouthwash. Then she smiled at her glowing reflection.

See how much better you feel now that the edge is off? she thought dreamily. *Now everything will be just fine.*

Down the hallway, Katie was scooping ice into the plastic bucket, thinking about her roommate. In her entire life she had never known anyone with Willow's looks, money, breeding, or family background.

It must be so great being her, Katie thought wistfully.

"Hi, there."

She whirled around.

Standing there grinning was the guy in the cowboy hat who had winked at her and Gigi in the hotel lobby. His hat was gone now, and she got a good look at him.

She guessed he was in his late teens. He was about five-foot-ten, slender but not skinny, with brown hair, radiant blue eyes, and one of the sweetest smiles Katie had ever seen.

But she couldn't pay attention to that now.

"I don't think guys are allowed on this floor," she said nervously.

He stepped back two or three paces and held his hands out to her, palms up. "I don't bite, I swear. It's just that the ice machine on the ninth floor is broken."

"Where's your ice bucket, then?" Katie asked.

He pointed behind her. "I left it there a minute ago when I went to the window to check out the view."

Sure enough, there was his ice bucket. Katie smiled at him sheepishly. "Sorry, I'm just . . . the pageant has all these rules."

"Pageant contestant, huh?"

She nodded.

"Where from?"

"Virginia," Katie replied.

"Miss Teen Spirit Virginia," he said, his accent-free voice belying the cowboy hat he'd had on earlier. "And a gorgeous credit to your state you are."

Katie blushed. Back in Virginia, she'd barely even dated; she spent so much time between her schoolwork and her after-school job at the video store that there wasn't time for dates, and certainly no money. And it wasn't like she was in the mood for renting a video and taking it home to watch with some guy after working in the store all evening.

Besides, she'd never really met a guy who seemed, well . . . really special.

"I'm from Back Bay, Virginia," Katie said. "It's a tiny, little town. We have to drive forty-five minutes to get to a movie theater."

"Yeah? Well, I'll look forward to hearing more about it over the next two weeks. I'm Dean Paisley. I'm with the pageant."

Katie froze. *Oh my gosh, this guy is a judge. Now he'll probably disqualify me for talking to a strange guy— him—in the hallway of the hotel. I bet it was a test of my moral character or something, and I blew it!*

"I'm really sorry, Mr. Paisley," she began to splutter. "I mean, I didn't mean to do whatever it was I wasn't supposed to do. I mean—"

Dean threw his head back and laughed. "You should see the look on your face! You can stop stammering, Miss Back Bay Virginia, I'm not one of the judges."

"You're not?"

"I'm not," Dean assured her. "I'm just the musical coordinator. And that's just a fancy title for rehearsal pianist, and then I get to sing during the pageant show. This is my tryout gig. If they like me, I get to stay with the pageant."

Country music, Katie decided. *That's why he was wearing that cowboy hat before.* She racked her brains for the name of a country artist she could mention. Maybe Dean wasn't a judge, but he sure was close to the judges. And it couldn't hurt.

A name came to her. Her mother had one country tape that she played over and over. "I like Martina McBride a lot."

"Ugh, country music," Dean said, grimacing. "Hate it."

"You hate . . . ?"

"Hate country, love Martina. And Victoria Shaw."

"But the cowboy hat . . ." Katie wondered aloud.

Dean grinned. "Mrs. Crownwell-Stevens likes that cowboy image for the Southern pageant. Hey, I'm a musician for hire, and I aim to please. By the way, what's your name, Miss Back Bay?"

"Katie Laramie."

Dean reached out his hand to shake hers. When their fingers met, the touch was electric. Katie blushed again, and hoped Dean couldn't tell.

"Well, Miss Katie Laramie Back Bay Virginia Teen Spirit," Dean said slowly, "I really shouldn't be saying this, but . . ."

"What?" Katie asked, mesmerized by his gorgeous blue eyes.

He grinned at her. "I hope you win."

Scarlett-Caress stood with her hands on her hips, scrutinizing Dawn. They were both ready to head downstairs for the opening dinner, and Scarlett-Caress wanted to make sure Dawn looked perfect.

"Hmmm," she mused. "The dress works with your coloring. The makeup is good; understated always works for the up-close stuff, but it's deadly under the stage lights.

Remember, you always do your makeup for the judges, not for the audience."

"Okay," Dawn agreed. "What else?"

Scarlett-Caress stroked her chin. "Let's see. Lose the pin, keep the necklace. Overaccessorizing is the kiss of death."

"Lose the pin," Dawn repeated as she unhooked the heart-shaped gold pin she was wearing from her dress. "Anything else, Madame Guru?"

"Just remember that you're brave and plucky at all times. You can really work that, what with your wheelchair and all. Believe me, the judges will eat it up with a spoon."

Dawn grimaced. "Yuck."

"Honey, you have to go with your strong suit. Like me, for example. I'm cute, of course, but I'm not drop-dead gorgeous. I've got a good body, but not a great body. And frankly, I'm not the greatest singer in the world, either. But I am friendly, sincere, and enthusiastic. I'm the all-American girl-next-door."

"But who are you, really?" Dawn wondered.

"What difference does it make?" Scarlett-Caress asked. "Oh, listen, just one more thing before we go downstairs." She sat on the edge of her bed, a serious look on her face. "There is a Virus amongst us."

"Come again?"

"Here at the pageant," Scarlett-Caress said solemnly. "That's capital 'V,' Virus. What is a Virus, you ask? A Virus is a pageant-head who is out to kill every other girl at the pageant."

Dawn just stared at her roommate. "I have no idea what you're talking about."

"Listen carefully," Scarlett-Caress instructed. "Her name is Allison Gaylord. She's Miss Southern Star. I've been in two other pageants with her, and my heart just fell through my Ferragamo pumps when I saw that she was here."

She looked at Dawn hard before continuing. "Watch out for her. She's got shoulder-length black hair, blue eyes, and a great figure. She's national baton-twirling champion in the under-eighteen category. If she gets a chance, she will use that baton to stab you in the back."

Dawn cocked her head at her roommate-turned-mentor. "This is a joke. Right?"

"Wrong. This is a girl who will do anything to win. In one pageant I was in two years ago, this terrific girl that everyone thought would win was disqualified when they found a tiny vodka bottle in her dance bag during rehearsal. We all knew Allison had put it there, but no one could prove it."

"Come on," Dawn scoffed. "That sounds like some bad TV movie."

"Well, it isn't. Another time she put Vaseline on this girl's toe shoes right before she went out to do her ballet number. The girl slid across the stage and sprained her ankle, and then she had to withdraw from the rest of the pageant."

Dawn was still dubious. "How do you know this girl Allison did it?"

"All the other girls in the pageant knew it was Allison," Scarlett-Caress insisted. "I'm telling you, this girl is evil. She might as well have six-six-six tattooed on her forehead." With that, she got up. "I'll point her out to you when you get downstairs."

"One last thing," Dawn said as they headed to the door. "What's that?"

"Did Allison actually win either of these pageants where she sabotaged the other girls?"

"She won one of them."

"And who won the other one?"

Scarlett-Caress flipped off the overhead light. "Me."

"You?"

"And she's never forgiven me for that either." Scarlett-Caress waited for Dawn to wheel herself into the hallway, and then closed the door behind them both. "So now I'm afraid The Virus thinks it's payback time."

CHAPTER

5

Katie and Willow were waiting for Gigi at the bank of elevators on their floor, when Katie suddenly remembered something.

"Willow?"

Her roommate turned to her, "Yes?"

"You didn't tell me the other favor."

Willow laughed. "You're right. Actually, I decided I didn't need to ask you. I mean, now that I see what a truly terrific person you are."

"That's so nice of you," Katie said.

Imagine a girl like Willow thinking that I'm terrific! That's something.

Willow put one slender hand on Katie's arm. "I just would really appreciate it if you wouldn't tell anyone about how sick I was."

"I won't say a thing," Katie promised.

Willow leaned over and kissed her cheek. "I feel so lucky to have gotten you as my roommate."

"Party time!" Gigi called out as she hurried over to them, Beth Kaplan in tow.

Gigi and Katie quickly introduced their roommates, then the four girls got into the glass elevator with six other pageant contestants from their floor. They could see all the way down to the ground floor as they got in. To their left and right were other elevators, all whooshing up and down silently.

"Katie, that dress is the bomb," Gigi assured her new friend.

"I look like a nun next to you," Katie said, laughing. Gigi had on a red dress with a short chiffon skirt.

"Well, I think all four of us look terrific," Willow told them warmly. "We each have our own style."

She is the most gracious person I ever met, Katie thought, marveling. *She's so totally in control, and I'm so nervous I'm afraid I'm getting sweat stains on my dress.*

The girls exited the elevator and followed the signs to the Donelson Room, where the dinner was being held. All the other contestants, chaperons, and invited guests were milling around, waiting for the banquet-room doors to open. Willow and Beth walked off to talk to some other girls as Dawn wheeled herself over to Gigi and Katie.

"Hey," she called, taking in their dresses. "Gosh, we all clean up nice, huh?"

"How's Scarlett-Caress?" Gigi asked.

"Well, bless your heart for asking," Dawn drawled, doing her best Scarlett-Caress imitation. "Actually, we seem to be having a sort of bizarre meeting of the minds."

"You mean you *like* her," Gigi was incredulous.

"Like wouldn't exactly be the right word," Dawn mused. "I'll tell you about it later. So, do y'all know what table you're at for dinner? There's a list over on that table."

Gigi, Katie, and Dawn made their way through the throng of buzzing girls and scanned the seating list for the dinner.

"You're at table fourteen," Gigi told Katie. "I'm at

seventeen with five total strangers who will soon come to love me, and Dawn is at nine with your roomie, Willow-the-Perfect. How is she, anyway?"

Katie shrugged. "Like you said, perfect."

"Dawn!" Scarlett-Caress called, hurrying over to her. "Ook-lay eehind-bay oo-yay," she whispered, cocking her head.

"That would be Martian for . . . ?" Dawn wondered.

"It's pig Latin for look behind you, silly," Scarlett-Caress whispered. "Call the Centers for Disease Control. The Virus is among us."

Dawn wheeled herself around. And found herself looking up at a beautiful, dark-haired girl in a white-and-blue linen suit, with a little American-flag pin in her lapel.

Allison Gaylord.

The Virus.

Allison's eyes swept over Dawn dismissively. Then she looked at Scarlett-Caress.

"Ohmigosh, Allison!" Scarlett-Caress cried in her best perky pageant voice. She rushed over to Allison and hugged her. "How fantastic to see you here!"

"How fantastic to see you here, too, Scarlett-Caress! Ohmigosh!" Allison gave Scarlett-Caress a huge hug in return. "Hey, isn't that Ashley Toups over there? I'll see you soon, Scarlett-Caress! Love you!" She rushed across the room to greet another girl just as warmly as she'd greeted Scarlett-Caress.

Scarlett-Caress leaned down to Dawn and whispered in her ear. "Don't say I didn't warn you," she singsonged.

"What was *that* about?" Gigi asked.

"That's another thing I'll tell you later," Dawn promised.

Just then two handsome, tuxedoed waiters flung open the doors to the banquet room, and everyone rushed to go inside.

"Talk to you later!" Gigi called as she headed for her assigned table. Her eyes swept the room, which had been decorated with all sorts of memorabilia from famous past scholarship pageants for girls. A huge forty-foot-square sign with the Teen Spirit logo in the corner read:

MISS TEEN SPIRIT
YEAR ONE, ALREADY #1!

Gigi found table 17—it was actually easy, since the tables all had big placards on them with their number. She sat down, and five other girls she hadn't yet met all joined her.

The girls quickly introduced themselves to each other.

One of them was Michelle Evans, Miss Southern Fitness, the only other African-American girl in the pageant.

I bet they put us at the same table so we could do that black-sister-bonding thing, Gigi thought, wanting to laugh aloud.

Michelle was tiny, slender, and muscular. She quickly told the other girls that she was a gymnast, and even though she hadn't yet started her senior year of high school, she had already been offered a gymnastics scholarship to Stanford University.

Then there was Wanda Sue Burnett, Miss Southern Beauty, who wore a short, slinky, low-cut purple dress that looked like it had been spray-painted on her amazing body. She didn't say much; she just kept checking to make sure her cleavage was perfectly aligned with the neckline of her dress.

There were two more girls, Jennifer Worden from South Carolina, and Becky Haas from Alabama. Becky was Miss Southern Brainiacs. Gigi knew Brainiacs was a national organization for teens with genius-level IQs.

And then there was redheaded Shyanne Derringer, Miss Southern Rodeo Queen, in her sequined cowgirl outfit.

"Your name isn't really Shyanne," Gigi said.

"For real, it is," Shyanne assured her.

"And you're a rodeo queen?" Michelle asked. "What is that?"

"Well, I do barrel racing and calf roping, and I do bareback tricks on my horse, Reba," Shyanne explained.

"Wow," said Wanda Sue, checking her cleavage again.

"How did you get started?" Becky asked.

"Oh, shoot"—Shyanne shrugged—"where I live in Marfa, Texas, we all start rodeoing when we're bitty things."

"Isn't Marfa where James Dean made the movie *Giant*?" Gigi asked.

"Danged tootin'!" Shyanne agreed proudly. "Are you a James Dean fan?"

Gigi grinned. "Well, he wasn't as hot as Will Smith, but he was hot."

"I brought the video with me, if you want to come watch it sometime," Shyanne offered eagerly. "I watch it at least once a week."

Becky shook her head. "You mean you brought a video of James Dean to the—"

At that moment a color guard carrying the Stars and Stripes and the state flag of Tennessee marched into the banquet room. Scarlett-Caress instantly jumped to her feet. All the other girls saw her, and they jumped to their feet as well. But it was Willow who reverently put her hand over her heart, out of respect for the flag. Quickly, at table after table, girls' hands dutifully rose to their hearts.

The color guard marched to the front of the auditorium, and Gigi recognized the cute guy who had winked at her and Katie in the lobby as he came forward to sing the National Anthem.

By the time he was done, there wasn't a dry eye in the room.

He's really good, Gigi thought. *I'd love to sing a duet with him. Strictly business, of course.*

She glanced over to Katie, at table 14. She could see that the other girl was gape-mouthed, her eyes shining, obviously impressed by the performance.

Or maybe by even more than the performance, Gigi thought impishly. *Actually, they'd make a cute couple.*

All the girls sat back down, in a rumbling of chairs.

And quickly, the empty seat at all the contestants' tables was filled by one of the judges.

Gigi gulped involuntarily. At her table, a rangy man in his late twenties had joined them.

"I'm Davis Nagel, and I play—"

"Oh, golly!" Shyanne interrupted him. "You're Davis Nagel!"

"I just said that." The man laughed. "I'm one of the judges. And we're going to have an informal chat now—nothing to be nervous about—which will count for part of your preliminary score."

Gigi had absolutely no idea who the man was, but from Shyanne's reaction, she had a feeling that she should have known.

"Y'all, this is Davis Nagel!" Shyanne said excitedly. "He plays quarterback for the Dallas Cowboys!"

"Second string," Davis added modestly.

"I am the biggest Cowboys fan in the world!" Shyanne cried. "Wait until I tell my daddy I met you!"

Gigi's heart sank as she listened. She knew nothing about professional football and cared about it even less. As she looked around the table the only girl besides Shyanne who seemed excited that Davis Nagel was one of the judges was

Becky Haas. Michelle and Wanda Sue looked as panicked as Gigi felt.

"Mr. Nagel, I saw the touchdown pass you threw in the game last year against Kansas City," Shyanne continued reverently. "You know, when they called holding on the play before and it was eight seconds left and fourth down and you threw the Hail Mary pass that won the game? My daddy called that poetry in motion."

"Hey, great!" Davis smiled in acknowledgment of her praise. "I was going to have you girls talk about your childhoods, but why don't we just talk football instead?"

Gigi's spirit fell even further.

"Only kidding." Davis grinned. "Okay, let's get started, girls." He looked directly at Gigi.

Gulp.

"Gigi—and thanks for wearing that name tag—what question would you want to ask me as we get this competition under way?"

Here was her chance to make a great first impression. But what could she say? Suddenly her mind, which usually worked overtime, was a complete blank.

Everyone at the table was staring at her, waiting.

And then, finally, it came to her.

"Well, Mr. Nagel, my father is a Baptist preacher, and I know he'd really appreciate my asking this question." She waited a long moment. "Exactly what *is* a Hail Mary pass?"

Davis burst out laughing. "You can't beat a truly great sense of humor, Gigi. Terrific!"

Gigi grinned back at him.

Her mom had always told her that anything you wanted to accomplish in life began with a dream.

Well, she could almost picture that Miss Southern Teen Spirit crown on her head. And after that, the nationals, where she'd get to sing on national TV. And after *that*, a recording contract with a major label.

That was her dream. And she believed with all her heart that her dream really could come true.

CHAPTER

"You know what I really, really want right now?" Katie announced as she chewed furiously on her sugarless gum. "A huge hot-fudge sundae. With nuts. And whipped cream. And an extra cherry."

"So, get one," Gigi said as she went through the tapes she had brought with her to find her favorite Aretha Franklin.

"Oh, right," Katie scoffed. "Tomorrow is our first dance rehearsal. I have to appear in front of everyone in tights. I might as well write 'blimp' across my thighs and call it a day."

"Ah, Aretha," Gigi breathed as the music came on. She began to dance around the room. "Now, here is a diva who does not worry about silly things like the size of her thighs."

It was Tuesday night. The day had seemed endless—long, private interviews with the panel of judges, plus the taping of a segment for a local TV talk show, plus a photo op with kids at a homeless shelter, and finally dinner with the mayor of Nashville.

And, all the time, the judges were watching them and taking notes.

Now it was after ten, and Katie and Dawn had come down to Gigi and Beth's room to hang out and discuss their day. The girls had already changed into pajamas, long T-shirts, or sweats. None of them wore any makeup and they all looked very young. Beth had even applied a purple facial mask called Essence of Herbs that was supposed to draw the impurities from her skin.

"R-E-S-P-E-C-T!" Gigi sang along with Aretha, using her hair pick as a make-believe microphone.

"Geeg, turn it down enough so we can think, huh?" Dawn yelled over the music.

Gigi obliged. "I learned to vocalize by singing along with Aretha. Someday I'm going to meet her and thank her for all that free training."

Dawn scrutinized Beth's purple face. "How long do you leave that gunk on?"

"The directions say thirty minutes," Beth replied. "It's supposed to give me a radiant glow."

Gigi opened Beth's jar of Essence of Herbs and sniffed. "Yuck. What's in this stuff, anyway?"

"Various aromatherapeutic healing herbs," Beth explained.

Gigi put the jar back on the nightstand. "It smells like my grandfather's compost heap." She took a running leap and landed between Katie and Beth on the bed. Beth was writing something in a notebook, and Gigi peered over her shoulder to see what it was.

"I'm charting how I think all the girls are doing so far," Beth explained.

"Girlfriend, you are a few slices short of a loaf," Gigi declared.

"How do you chart something like that?" Dawn asked.

"I realize it's all subjective on my part," Beth admitted. "My judgments might be different from the actual judges. But I try to put myself in their shoes."

"So, who do we all think is hot stuff?" Gigi asked. "Besides us, of course."

"That's easy. Willow Rose Harrison," Beth said.

Dawn nodded. "I second that. What do you think, Katie? She's your roommate."

"She's great," Katie said.

Beth tapped her pen against her pad of paper. "Not just great. Perfect, as far as I can see."

"Okay, I grant you she's beyond gorgeous," Gigi began.

"And smart and graceful and gracious," Beth added.

"Very Grace Kelly," Dawn said, nodding.

Gigi reached for her nail polish on the nightstand and opened the bottle. "Who's Grace Kelly?"

"She was this gorgeous American actress who married the Prince of Monaco and became a princess," Dawn explained.

Katie nodded. "That's what Willow has. She has the look of royalty."

"Well, maybe she doesn't have any talent," Gigi suggested as she applied a coat of shimmery beige nail polish.

"And maybe her school grades are bad," Beth added. "Or she hasn't done enough community service. Remember, Grace Kelly died in a car wreck."

"Almost straight A's in advanced classes, tons of volunteer work," Katie informed them.

"And she's, what, a singer?" Dawn asked. "I suppose she sings like an angel, too."

"That I don't know," Katie said. "I haven't heard her sing yet. But she worked with Céline Dion's vocal coach, I know that much."

Everyone was quiet for a moment, absorbing all this information.

"Well, maybe she has some awful secret character flaw." Gigi waved her nails around to dry them.

Maybe she does, Katie thought. *Maybe she drinks.*

"So, what's the poop on her, Katie?" Gigi pressed. "You live with her."

Katie shrugged. "She's really terrific."

Gigi playfully hit Katie with a pillow. "Oh, that's *real* helpful."

"I would also have to rate Wanda Sue Burnett a ten on looks," Beth said.

"Do you think those breasts are the real thing?" Dawn asked.

"I'll ask her tomorrow," Gigi announced, "in front of all the judges." They all cracked up.

"What about Scarlett-Caress?" Beth asked. "I think she's definitely a contender."

"Well, bless your heart for saying so." Gigi mimicked Scarlett-Caress's gushing manner. "How can you stand living with her, Dawn?"

Dawn laughed. "I know you're all gonna think I'm crazy, but . . . I like her."

"No!" Katie exclaimed.

"Yes," Dawn said. "Oh, you guys, listen to this! Scarlett-Caress told me that Allison Gaylord is out to ruin any girl in this pageant that she thinks might have a chance of winning."

"Who's Allison Gaylord?" Katie wondered.

"Dark hair, really pretty, from Texas?" Dawn reminded her. "She's the one who made sure she was standing front and center when they took that group shot of us with the kids at the homeless shelter this afternoon."

"Oh, right." Gigi nodded. "She was standing right in front of Michelle Evans, and Michelle is so tiny you couldn't even see her."

"Wait until I tell you what else Scarlett-Caress told me

about Allison," Dawn said. Then she proceeded to inform them about The Virus.

"Oh, come on," Katie scoffed. "I don't believe that."

"I do," Gigi said.

"I don't have enough facts to make a decision about it yet," Beth put in. She padded into the bathroom to wash off her facial mask.

Gigi stretched out on her stomach. "Now that I think about it, I saw Allison flirting with Dean Paisley at the dinner tonight."

"When?" Dawn asked.

"Right after they cleared away dessert," Gigi said. "They were standing over by the piano in the corner, and she kept fluttering her eyelashes at him. She's too smart to actually touch him, I guess. Not in public, anyway."

"Pageant Rule number forty-five: No Teen Spirit contestant shall make physical contact with any male who is not a family member," Dawn recited solemnly. "Dean *is* really cute, though, I have to admit."

"Not as cute as Trey, but cute," Gigi agreed. She grinned impishly. "I think he's got a thing for Katie."

"He does not," Katie protested, blushing.

"He sat with you at dinner, didn't he?" Gigi pointed out.

"I'm sure he got assigned to sit at my table, that's all. And the seat next to me happened to be empty, so—"

"So you want him bad," Gigi teased her.

"I do not!" Katie insisted, turning even redder. "I don't even know him!"

"She's only teasing you," Dawn told Katie. "You act like you've never had a boyfriend in your life!"

Katie didn't say a word.

"You mean you really haven't?" Dawn asked.

"Haven't what?" Beth asked as she returned to the room with her freshly washed face.

"Had a boyfriend," Dawn explained.

"Not really," Katie admitted, looking down at the quilted bedspread.

"Next thing you're gonna tell us you're a virgin." Gigi guffawed

Once again, Katie didn't say a word.

Gigi scrambled up on to her knees. "Wait, you're seventeen and you're still a virgin?"

"So am I," Dawn said. "What's wrong with that?"

Gigi fell over laughing. "Nothing! I'm a virgin, too! I just always think I'm the only one!"

As they were speaking Beth had lain down on the floor, where she was now doing leg lifts. "Not me," she said as she changed legs.

Everyone looked at her with their mouths hanging open.

"Were you in love?" Katie finally asked.

"Not really," Beth answered as she continued her leg lifts. "I decided virginity would only get in the way of both my short-term and long-term goals."

"How?" Katie asked, fascinated.

"All my friends think about sex and love and guys all the time," Beth explained, turning onto her back and beginning to do sit-ups. "Well, I don't want my focus to be on romance. It's too distracting. So I picked out a guy in whom I had no romantic interest, even though he was quite attractive, and . . . we did it."

"Someone at an institute ought to study you," Gigi murmured.

"What was it like?" Katie wondered.

"That is something every girl has to find out for herself," Beth said. She sat up. "Did anyone keep track of how many sit-ups I just did? I need to chart it."

Gigi screamed and threw a pillow at Beth, then Katie bopped Gigi with another pillow, and Dawn grabbed the first pillow from Beth and bopped Katie. Soon they were all screaming and laughing, having a huge pillow fight.

There was a loud, insistent knock on their door.

"Girls, girls! It's Mrs. Drummond!"

The girls all froze, breathing hard. Mrs. Drummond was Gigi and Beth's chaperon, and her room was right next door. Mrs. Drummond was already notorious for being the oldest and strictest of all the chaperons.

"Yes, Mrs. Drummond?" Gigi called sweetly.

"What is all the noise in there?" the chaperon demanded. "Open this door at once!"

Beth went to the door and opened it. "Yes, Mrs. Drummond?"

"Those were not ladylike noises I heard coming from this room!"

"Actually, Mrs. Drummond, we were practicing our vocal exercises to prepare for the opening number where we'll all be singing," Beth explained, straight-faced.

"I see," Mrs. Drummond replied stiffly. "You'll need to practice more quietly in the future."

Beth nodded. "Thank you for pointing that out to us, Mrs. Drummond."

"Bed check is in twenty minutes," she reminded Beth, then she marched back to her room.

Beth shut the door. "From now on, ladylike noises only, please."

At that moment Gigi belched as loudly as she could, which sent all the girls into gales of laughter. They did their best to smother these with their ladylike hands.

CHAPTER

7

"Tell me the truth. Just how fat do I look in this?" Katie asked Dawn as she walked and Dawn wheeled into the large room where dance rehearsal was taking place the next morning.

Dawn, who was wearing gray-and-white polkadot leggings with a gray-and-white polkadot sports bra, took in her friend's shimmery blue leotard and baggy blue sweatpants.

"You look fine," she concluded.

"The sweatpants don't look stupid?" Katie pressed nervously. "Because I'm wearing them to hide my thighs."

"Nah," Dawn said. "You just look like you're secure enough to not have to flaunt your body around."

"Oh, that's great." Katie sighed with relief and then noticed Allison Gaylord hurrying by with Donna Juarez, another girl from Texas.

Allison had on pale pink biker shorts over a scoop-necked pale pink leotard with spaghetti straps. Her perfectly aerobicized arms were bare. A matching pale pink ribbon tied back her glossy, dark hair.

"She's in perfect shape," Katie noted with a sigh.

"Michelle Evans told me there's a group of girls that gets up at five o'clock in the morning to work out, and Allison's always the first one there."

"Willow does, too," Katie said as they entered the rehearsal room. "I know I should, but I just feel so self-conscious with those girls!"

"Hey, Katie! How's it going?" Dean asked, striding over to them.

"Everything's fine," Katie said.

"Great." Dean grinned at her. "I'm accompanying you guys at your choreography rehearsal."

"Maybe I could just lie across your piano draped with a feather boa while they dance," Dawn suggested.

Dean laughed. "I'm afraid it's a medley of patriotic songs. Not exactly feather-boa material."

He is so darling, Katie thought, for maybe the zillionth time since she had met him. *He was so sweet to me at dinner last night. But there are so many girls here who are cuter than me, he couldn't actually like me. Could he?*

"So, Miss Back Bay, how's your hoofing?" Dean asked.

"My dancing, you mean? Frankly, terrible," Katie confessed. "The only thing I do worse than dance is sing—and we have to do that in the production number, too!"

"You see, that's what I like about you," Dean said. "So many of the girls here are so fake and full of themselves. You, Katie Laramie, are a real person. And a cute one, at that."

"Hey, watch it," Dawn teased, ostentatiously looking around the lobby. "If a chaperon sees you flirting with my friend here, you'll both get tossed out."

Dean raised his hands, palms up. "Both my hands are clearly visible to every passing pageant official. I was merely making polite conversation." He took one step closer to Katie. "Not that I wouldn't like to do much more," he added, his voice low and sexy.

Now he took a step away from them, and said in a much louder voice, "See you in there."

"Wow," Dawn said, as she and Katie watched Dean walk away.

"He's really nice," Katie admitted.

"He's really *hot*," Dawn corrected.

Katie smiled self-consciously. "He's both."

Katie walked and Dawn wheeled herself into the huge ballroom that had been set up for their rehearsal. At the other end of the room was a large stage. To one side was a grand piano with sheet music on it.

"I can't believe I have to sing and dance," Katie moaned, watching Allison, Scarlett-Caress, and Michelle confidently warming up onstage. "When Mrs. Crownwell-Stevens sees how bad I am, she's going to kick me out of the pageant!"

Dawn put her hand on Katie's arm. "Whoa, Katie, look over there at Wanda Sue! Can you believe what she's wearing?"

Wanda Sue Burnett was standing near the rear wall, staring at her face in the mirror of her compact. She had on a leopard-print thong leotard that appeared to have a built-in push-up bra.

"If she tries to dance, her breasts are going to smack her in the face!" Dawn giggled to Katie.

"Okay, girls, let's hustle!" Jimmy Delancy, their choreo-grapher, called from the stage. "I want all of you up here, pronto."

All the contestants dutifully climbed up onto the stage. No one had thought to make a ramp for Dawn's wheelchair, so Dean and Jimmy had to lift her in her chair.

"Gee, I love the service," Dawn quipped as they set her chair down.

"How many of you have had any dance training?" Jimmy asked.

Almost everyone's hand shot into the air.

"I'm not talking about weenie stuff to fill up your pageant résumé," Jimmy told them. "I mean real stuff. And don't try to con me, because I'll find out the truth soon enough."

Scarlett-Caress's hand went in the air, as did Allison's, Michelle's, and four other girls'.

"Okay, real dancers down in front. The rest of you make two lines behind them."

The girls shuffled around onstage.

From the side of the stage, Dawn's heart hammered in her chest. This was what she had been dreading. In her stage pageant, there hadn't been any group numbers to perform.

You can do this, she told herself.

She wheeled herself over to the choreographer.

"Where would you like me?" Dawn asked, trying to sound calm and confident.

Jimmy Delancy stared at her blankly.

"You remember me," Dawn said helpfully. "The one you just hoisted up here."

"Yeah, of course," the choreographer agreed.

He forgot all about having to work me into the dance numbers, Dawn realized. *He hasn't given it a second's thought.*

"So . . . what's your name, again?" Jimmy asked.

"Dawn Faison."

"Right, right. Okay, Dawn, you stay right here for now. I'll work you into the number." He started to walk away, then turned back to Dawn. "Do the hand gestures I teach, okay?"

She nodded her agreement.

For the next hour Jimmy took them through a series of dance combinations, first without music, then with Dean on the piano. From time to time various judges wandered into the back of the room and watched them.

"You in the second row, in the white leotard," Jimmy called. "Step forward. What's your name?"

Willow took a step forward. "Willow."

"You move like a dream, Willow. Step in the center of the front line of dancers."

"That's very kind of you," Willow said. "But I've only had one year of jazz and two years of ballet."

"Hey, if you've got it, you've got it." Jimmy shrugged, grinning. "And you've got it. Okay, girls, let's take it from the top one more time. With the music, Dean."

Dean nodded as Jimmy counted to four and the girls went through the dance steps again. Over to the side, all by herself, Dawn dutifully did the hand gestures.

I feel like an idiot, she thought miserably as she raised her hands over her head and shook her fingers.

"Okay, last eight bars!" Jimmy called over the music. "And hustle, two-three-four, turn, two-three-four, pose-and-smile, three-four, and hold."

The girls were breathing hard. Some took sips from their water bottles. Others wiped off sweat with a towel.

Jimmy threw up his hands in disgust. "No, no, no! You girls in the back row, what's the problem? We're not even halfway through this number, and you're moving like you're paralyzed from the waist down!"

A sudden hush descended on the room. Everyone's eyes slid over to Dawn.

Jimmy turned to her and hit himself in the forehead, declaring, "I'm a jerk."

"It's all right," Dawn said, trying to maintain her composure.

"Excuse me, Mr. Delancy," Scarlett-Caress called.

"What is it?"

"Well, I think it's just so incredibly brave of Dawn to be here, what with her physical challenges and all. And I think we need to show the true meaning of Miss Teen Spirit by making her a real part of this dance number."

Katie noticed that three of the judges were standing in the back of the room, hearing every word of Scarlett-Caress's seemingly generous speech. They murmured to each other, nodding, and looked at the girl with admiration.

"No, no, that's okay." Dawn smiled weakly. "I'm fine right here. Really."

Jimmy rubbed his jaw. "What's your name?" he asked Scarlett-Caress.

She told him sweetly.

"Well, Scarlett-Caress, you're absolutely right."

"We think so, too!" Allison cried dramatically, taking a step forward. "In fact, Dawn should be *featured* in this dance number. Don't y'all agree?"

Most of the girls offered loud endorsements of the idea. Katie and Gigi traded looks. Neither of them thought Dawn would be very happy being the token crippled girl featured in their dance number.

"Here's what we'll do," Jimmy said, thinking as he spoke. "Dawn, wheel yourself center, please. In the front row."

Willow moved over as Dawn reluctantly wheeled herself into her spot.

"Now we'll change the formations a little, and make it more like the spokes of a wheel, with Dawn at the center," Jimmy continued. "Dawn, when the girls go around, you'll turn your wheelchair in a circle. Got that?"

Red-faced with humiliation, Dawn nodded.

Tentatively, from the back row, Katie's hand went into the air.

Jimmy sighed. "What now?"

Katie nervously cleared her throat. "Well, I was thinking

that maybe you could choreograph part of the number where all of us are sitting down, doing the choreography with our hands and faces. Or . . . or with hand props or something. It could be cute, I think. Then Dawn wouldn't be the only one sitting down, and then—"

"How many choreographers do you see in this room?" Jimmy interrupted, his hands on his hips.

"One," Katie said meekly.

"That's right, one. And that choreographer is perfectly capable of choreographing this number without help from a girl in the back row with two left feet!"

Katie stared at the floor, horribly embarrassed.

"Okay, ladies, back to work." Jimmy clapped his hands briskly. "And I mean really work this time!"

They danced for two more hours. During the entire number, Dawn was front and center, often wheeling around in a circle. To her enormous chagrin, the dance ended with all the girls on one knee waving little American flags while she sat in front of them wearing a fake Uncle Sam white beard that hooked on behind her ears, holding a large American flag.

When the rehearsal finally broke up, Allison Gaylord came rushing over to Dawn. She leaned down and hugged her.

"You were so wonderful!" Allison cried. "And you look so cute with that little white beard on, really!"

Dawn felt tears of humiliation fill her eyes. She willed them back. "I didn't do anything."

"Oh, don't be so modest," Allison chided, and started to walk away. Then she noticed that two judges were still in the back of the room, so she turned back to Dawn and raised her voice, to make sure the judges would hear her. "And Dawn, if there's anything I can do for you at any time—you just call on me!"

"Drop dead," Dawn said under her breath.

Scarlett-Caress hurried over. "The Virus will help you, all right," she said, watching as Allison walked to the back of the room to chat with the judges. "She'll help you into an early grave."

She turned back to Dawn. "So, notice how I got you center stage, roomie. Feel free to thank me profusely."

"I didn't *want* to be center stage," Dawn gritted, trying to control her anger. "I look like a total idiot wheeling around in a circle center stage, and it's your fault."

Scarlett-Caress was aghast. "Dawn, I was *helping* you!"

"You were not," Dawn said. "You were helping yourself. You thought the judges would eat up what you said—to use your words—with a spoon. And I bet they did, Scarlett-Caress."

"Good." Scarlett-Caress put her hands on her hips. "Then I helped both of us. That was the general idea."

"I don't need any more of your so-called help, okay?" Dawn snapped. She began to wheel herself away from her roommate. "From now on, just leave me the hell alone!"

"Hello?"

"Kelly? It's me."

"Dawn!" Kelly screamed happily. "You haven't even called me since you got there! I've been dying to hear everything. Is it fabulous?"

After the humiliating dance rehearsal, Dawn had hurried up to her room. Fortunately, Scarlett-Caress had gone to the lobby for cold drinks with Shyanne, Michelle, and Willow, so she had the room to herself.

Tears were spilling down Dawn's cheeks as she spoke into the phone. "It sucks."

Kelly Madison had been Dawn's best friend forever. Kelly had been with her the day of the accident, and she had stuck by Dawn through everything. In fact, it was Kelly who had badgered and badgered her about entering the Miss Teen Spirit Mississippi contest in the first place.

"Did something bad happen?" Kelly asked with concern.

"It's just everything," Dawn said, fisting the tears off her cheeks.

"Like what?"

Dawn proceeded to tell Kelly all about the horrible dance number, and how a lot of the girls treated her as if she were both a saint and mentally retarded at the same time.

"And I hate it all," she concluded, blowing her nose into a tissue. "I have no idea what I'm doing here."

"You're competing, just like every other girl there."

Dawn sighed into the phone. "Oh, Kel, I don't belong here. I'm so tired of putting on this brave act and having everyone tell me how much they admire me."

"There are worse things than being admired," Kelly said.

"You know what I mean! I just want to be treated like everyone else, and that's never going to happen. I'm not the poster girl for cripples, okay? I'm . . . I'm thinking about dropping out."

There was silence on the other end of the phone.

"Kel? You still there?"

"Uh-huh."

"Well, say something," Dawn demanded.

"I don't know what to say," Kelly admitted. "I mean, I don't think you should drop out. I think you have to stay and see it through."

"Give me one good reason why I should."

"Because you've never been a quitter, Dawn."

Dawn could feel fury welling up inside of her. "That's easy for you to say, isn't it?"

"Look, I'm sorry you're not having fun, Dawn, but don't take it out on me."

"Why not? This whole pageant thing was your idea!"

"I know that, but—oh, my gosh, I am so late," Kelly said. "I just looked at the time, Dawn. I've got to go."

"How come?"

"Sean and Josh and Connie are on their way over. We're going hiking on the Old Natchez Trace."

Hearing this, Dawn's fury grew. Josh and Connie were a couple and had been for over a year. Sean was Sean Kingsley. The same Sean she had been trying to impress three years earlier when she'd accepted his dare, climbed up the high rock, slipped, and broken her neck.

The same Sean that only Kelly knew Dawn still secretly loved.

After I was paralyzed, Sean never paid any attention to me at all, she thought bitterly. *It was like once I couldn't walk, I wasn't even a girl anymore.*

"Are you and Sean together now?" Dawn asked, her voice tight.

"Dawn, you know we're just buds."

"Really? Because it sounds like two couples are going hiking together," Dawn said.

"Dawn, you're my best friend in the world," Kelly said earnestly. "I know how you feel about Sean. I would never—"

"Why not? He'd never look at me now. He's made that pretty clear."

"We're not the only four people on this hike, Dawn. Carol and her sister are coming, and Ben Jacobs and—"

"Sounds like fun," Dawn snapped.

Kelly sighed. "You sound like you're really, really ticked at me and I don't even know why. But, look, I can't talk anymore now or I'm going to be late. How about if I call you—"

Dawn slammed down the phone.

Instantly she regretted it.

But even as tears poured down her cheeks she didn't call Kelly back to apologize.

I'm sick of being nice and understanding and noble, she thought. *I'm sick of my friends going hiking together when I can't even walk. I'm sick of being patronized and humiliated, of watching guys like Dean flirt with girls like Katie right in front of me like I don't even exist. No one flirts with me, ever.*

Dawn's sobs grew even louder as she pummeled the sides of her chair. "I hate you!" she yelled. "I hate you!"

Even Dawn didn't know if she was talking to the wheelchair, or to herself.

CHAPTER

"I just love to swim!" Wanda Sue Burnett cooed to Katie from her seat across the tour-bus aisle. "Don't you?"

"Sure," Katie agreed, doing her best to smile back.

Swimming! she thought in a panic. *I can't believe they're taking us all swimming. If there was a swimsuit competition in this pageant, I never would have entered. And now they're taking us swimming, and all the judges will see me in a bathing suit, anyway!*

"It's just a media photo op," Scarlett-Caress observed laconically as she examined one of her perfectly manicured fingers and the tour bus slowly rumbled along in the late-morning tourist traffic that snarled Briley Parkway outside the Opryland Hotel complex. She was sitting next to Wanda Sue and looking idly at the passing scenery.

"What's wrong with media photo opportunities?" Wanda Sue asked self-righteously.

"Not a thing, sweetums," Scarlett-Caress told her.

"I happen to like the camera," Wanda Sue said.

"And I'm sure it's extremely fond of you, too," Gigi told her, leaning across Katie.

It was late the next morning. The coordinating committee had noted that the temperature that day was supposed to hit one hundred degrees, so they had scheduled a trip to Wave Country, a huge outdoor pool near the old Opryland amusement park, for a swim break. And photos, of course.

After that, they would have a rehearsal of their platform speeches—without the judges—and following *that*, they'd be whisked off to a catfish dinner at one of Nashville's most famous catfish-and-barbecue restaurants, Tastebuds.

The dinner was something most of the girls were looking forward to, because it would be a joint event with the Future Fellows, a group of high-school seniors from all across the state of Tennessee who'd been chosen to spend a week of intensive leadership training at Tennessee State University. Rumor had it that more than half of the Future Fellows were guys. This would be one of the few events that would allow the Miss Teen Spirit contestants to be anywhere *near* guys.

Like everything else at the pageant, this swimming trip was meticulously planned, right down to the front five seats of the bus piled high with fluffy white towels embossed with the gold Miss Teen Spirit logo, and matching containers of SPF-30 sunblock.

"Girls, your attention, please!" Mrs. Crownwell-Stevens called over the bus's loudspeaker. "Please make sure you stay with the group at all times. Under no circumstances are you allowed to speak with strangers. We've rented out Wave Country for two hours, so no one should be in the pool besides you girls. However, you can never be too careful out in public. Also, I'm sure you all remember that no two-piece bathing suits are allowed. This information was explicitly spelled out in the pageant handbook, but a reminder is always helpful."

"Why don't we all just wear granny gowns and veils?" Gigi griped to Katie.

"That would be better than having the judges see me in a bathing suit," Katie whispered back.

"Y'all, I sure hope my tan lines don't show in the photos." Shyanne sounded worried.

"Don't you know anything?" Allison asked from the seat behind her. "Never tan with a bathing suit on before a pageant."

"No one ever told me that," Shyanne replied, crestfallen.

"Well, if you had half a brain you would have figured it out yourself," Allison retorted. "In the history of beauty pageants, no girl with tan lines has ever been in the finals."

At that moment one of the judges, Molly Cantor, who was an agent at the William Morris Agency, moved down the aisle and stopped in front of them. "How's it going today, girls?"

"Oh, just terrific!" Allison chirped. "We were all just saying how sweet it is for the pageant to arrange for us to go swimming on such a hot day."

"I wish I could put on my suit and join you," Molly said, smiling, "but I'm afraid the sight of me in a bathing suit would scare everyone out of the water."

"Oh, poo!" Allison said. "You look like you work out all the time!"

The bus pulled up outside the main gate of Wave Country. Instantly, a couple of uniformed attendants stepped onto the bus to help unhook Dawn's wheelchair from its tethers in the back as the rest of the girls reached into the luggage racks above their heads for the travel bags that held their swimwear.

"Remember, girls," Mrs. Crownwell-Stevens cautioned over the loudspeaker of the bus, "you are representing *Teen Spirit* magazine and the Miss Teen Spirit Pageant here today. I'm sure all of you will conduct yourselves appropriately. Now go have fun . . . and be natural! Don't worry about the judges for the next hour or so. Mrs. Drummond will be accompanying them over to the Opryland Hotel for a quick tour, which should give you ladies a breather. Smile for the photographers and the videographers, stay cool, and please . . . nobody drown unnecessarily."

With this last word, everyone laughed as a huge cheer went up when the girls realized that they'd be swimming without the attention of the ever-present judges. Even Willow Rose and Scarlett-Caress joined in. It would be the first time that all the contestants had been together without the judges present, and everyone was relieved.

Thank God, Katie thought. *I have been rescued from having the judges see me in a bathing suit.*

The girls all got off the bus and were quickly ushered into a private area that had been reserved for them. There were private changing booths with lit vanity mirrors and every toiletry item anyone could ever think of.

"Dang, I never saw a Wave Country like this one." Shyanne marveled. "It's real nice, huh?"

"They don't supply this to everyone, you twit," Allison told her. "It's just for us."

Shyanne reddened with embarrassment.

"You don't have to be so nasty to her," Beth told Allison.

"You know, you're right. God already did that when he gave her an IQ with two digits in it."

Shyanne looked like she was ready to cry.

"Come on, Shyanne," Beth said, taking the other girl's arm. "I want to tell you why it is that Allison Gaylord wins so few of the hundreds of pageants she enters. Have you ever heard of the laws of karma?"

The girls quickly changed into their bathing suits and slowly gathered near the Wave Country snack bar. Many of them felt they had to redo their hair or makeup, or cover their bodies with waterproof body makeup, before going out to the photo shoot.

The photographers, meanwhile, were being kept back in a group about thirty yards away from them by the pageant organizers and chaperons. Another pageant organizer handed out sunblock and towels as one by one, the girls trickled outside.

"Gigi, you look great!" Katie told her as they got their sunblock and towel.

Gigi had on a red bathing suit with high-cut legs.

"Well, you keep talking about these fat thighs of yours, and I don't see any fat on you," Gigi replied.

"Ha." Katie looked down at herself in her black Lycra suit covered with sunflowers.

"Katie, that suit is just the cutest," Allison said, coming over to her.

"Thanks," Katie said warily.

"It's really very slimming around the hips and thighs," Allison went on. "It must be so hard to find a decent suit when you're so small on the top and so huge on the bottom, huh? Can't you afford to get some liposuction or something?"

"I—" Katie began, determined to defend herself.

"Oh! There's Willow," Allison cried before Katie could complete a phrase. "I've got to run over and say hello."

"Maybe Scarlett-Caress was right about her," Katie said, fuming. "She really *is* The Virus."

Gigi put on her red sunglasses. "I've got her number. When no judges or pageant officials are around, she's a total witch. When they *are* around, she's Miss Sunshine."

As Gigi walked off to talk to Beth, Dawn wheeled herself over to Katie.

"You going to be okay with this swimming?" Katie asked her.

"I'm fine," Dawn said tersely.

"Is something wrong?" Katie asked. It seemed to her as if Dawn had been acting weird all morning.

"I've just got a lot on my mind," Dawn said, putting on her sunglasses. "I'm thinking about . . . well, let's just say I've got a decision to make."

"About the pageant?"

Dawn nodded.

"Do you want to talk about it?"

"There's nothing to talk about. I hate it here."

Katie knelt down so that her face was at the same level as Dawn's. "You're not thinking about dropping out, are you?"

"Get up," Dawn snapped. "I hate it when people kneel down to me like I'm a little kid."

Katie stood up. "I'm sorry. Well, if you just want to be left alone, I understand." She started to walk away.

"Katie, wait," Dawn called to her. She wheeled herself toward her friend. "I'm sorry. I'm the one who should be apologizing to you. You're really great, Katie. You and Gigi are the only two good things about being here."

"I know that dance rehearsal yesterday was awful for you."

Dawn nodded. "I keep thinking, why am I putting myself through this? I don't have to prove anything to anybody. I really do think I'm going to quit."

Katie put her hand on Dawn's arm. "I wish you wouldn't."

"Why?"

"Because I'd miss you," she said simply. "So would Gigi. And a lot of the other girls, too, for that matter. Everyone here isn't two-faced."

"I know that."

"Besides, you *deserve* to be here," Katie continued. "You earned it just as much—maybe more—than any of us."

Dawn smiled ironically. "You know what's funny, Katie?"

"What?"

"The one reason you *didn't* give for why I should stay in the pageant."

Katie looked confused. "What's that?"

"Can't you guess?" Dawn asked. "It's the reason that The Virus is nice to me, and Scarlett-Caress gives me all these great pageant tips, and so many of the other girls tell me how brave and plucky I am until I want to throw up."

Dawn took a deep breath. "Being sweet to the crippled girl is easy, because every single one of you knows *I won't win.*

"And that," she concluded sadly, "is the biggest insult of all."

Mrs. Crownwell-Stevens's assistant had checked all the girls' names off on her list, except one. "Where's Wanda Sue Burnett?" the young girl called out.

Everyone looked around.

At that moment Wanda Sue emerged from the dressing-room area. Clearly she had waited until the last possible moment so she could make an eye-catching entrance.

Every head turned to her, and every eye popped.

When the photographers saw her in her one-piece silver lamé bathing suit, with the legs cut up to her waist, and the front cut down to her navel, they couldn't hold themselves back. They ran from their holding area toward Wanda Sue, and started snapping away.

Flat-chested, muscular Michelle stared bullets at the other girl's cleavage. "Oh, this is just great."

"This way, Wanda Sue!" a photographer called to the girl as the others jostled for position.

Wanda Sue obliged, bending over a little so more of her amazing cleavage was visible to all.

"She's not Miss Teen Spirit, she's a future Miss November," Gigi decided. "So I say, let's go swimming."

En masse, except for Wanda Sue, the girls headed for the pool, even Allison and Scarlett-Caress, leaving Wanda Sue behind with the photographers.

She didn't seem to mind at all.

"Your platform speech was precious," Scarlett-Caress told Dawn as the two of them waited in their room for Gigi and Katie to come and meet them. They were all ready to leave for the catfish dinner at Tastebuds.

Dawn didn't say anything. She was staring out the window of their room, watching the traffic whiz by on the interstate across the Cumberland River.

I felt so certain I was going to drop out this morning, Dawn mused. *But then when I got a chance to rehearse my platform speech in front of all the other girls this afternoon, I really got into it. And now . . . now I don't know what I want to do.*

"Oh, come on," Scarlett-Caress was saying. "You can't still be mad at me about the choreography thing, can you?"

"Yes, I can," Dawn said, wheeling herself around. "It was humiliating."

Scarlett-Caress shook her head. "Honey, there is no room for humiliation at a pageant. You have to use what you've got. Haven't you learned anything at all from me yet?"

"You're as bad as The Virus," Dawn snapped.

Scarlett-Caress put her hands over her heart. "Now, I am truly wounded by that."

"Don't be. There's no room for wounded at a pageant."

Scarlett-Caress seemed to think about this for a minute. "You're right. I'll just learn from this experience. From now on, I'll only give you pageant tips in private. How would that be?"

"Precious," Dawn replied.

Scarlett-Caress laughed. "*Now* you're gettin' it! And I meant what I said about your platform speech. Helping Hands sounds like a wonderful organization. And to think, you're the person who started it."

"I'll tell you how I got the idea," Dawn said, getting excited in spite of herself. "I was tutoring this girl in math, and she didn't have much money. So she asked me if we could work out a trade. She'd help me out with stuff I couldn't do physically and I'd help her out academically by tutoring her. It worked out really well. I mean, I felt really good that I could help her, and she felt really good that she could help me."

"Makes sense to me," Scarlett-Caress said, nodding.

"So then I thought, what if there was an organization that matched teens with physical challenges and teens with academic challenges. I mean, it would be a win-win situation for everyone, right?"

"Right!" Scarlett-Caress agreed.

"So . . . I started it. I decided to call it Helping Hands. In my hometown, Starkville, Mississippi, fifty-six high-school and Mississippi State University students signed up in the first three months. And after that, it just grew and grew."

"And now there are six chapters of Helping Hands around the country." There was real respect in Scarlett-Caress's eyes. "I just admire you so much, Dawn. I really do."

For a moment Dawn felt truly good about herself. "Thanks. Your speech was good, too."

"Yawn," Scarlett-Caress replied, lolling on her bed. "My platform is Special Olympics. Who's against Special Olympics? Exactly no one. Which is exactly why I chose it."

Dawn laughed. She couldn't help marveling at Scarlett-Caress's uncanny understanding of the psychology of pageants.

It was funny—when she was alone with Katie or Gigi or even Scarlett-Caress, all her anger about the pageant seemed to disappear. It was only when she was participating in the events themselves that she found herself wanting to quit.

That afternoon, all of the contestants had rehearsed their platform speeches in front of all the other girls. So now everyone knew everyone else's platform. Later on in the competition, they'd each give their speeches in front of the judges, who'd have the opportunity to pepper them with questions. Platform speeches and community service were heavily emphasized in this pageant.

"Now don't get mad," Scarlett-Caress began, "but I have a couple of teeny little suggestions for you."

"Such as?" Dawn asked warily.

"Well, I was watching you," the other girl said. "If I were you, I'd get out from behind that little wheelchair-height podium they made for you as much as I could. It makes you look ridiculous."

"I *felt* ridiculous," Dawn admitted.

"You've got a wireless mike, so just wheel yourself out. The judges need to see the wheelchair at all times. Never give them a chance to forget about your condition." Scarlett-Caress paused for emphasis then continued.

"And another thing." She pointed to the side of Dawn's wheelchair. "You need some props."

"Props?"

"Absolutely," Scarlett-Caress said. "When you get to the part in your speech where you talk about teaching that girl wheelchair tennis, you need to bring out a racquet and balls, and show those judges how you serve."

"And hit a judge in the head with a tennis ball," Dawn said wryly.

"Honey, serve toward *off*stage," Scarlett-Caress said sweetly.

Dawn considered this idea for a moment. Her roommate was right. It was an incredible idea. And no one else would do it, that's for sure.

"Scarlett-Caress, thanks—"

"Don't thank me," Scarlett cut her off. "You would have figured it out on your own in three or four pageants. I'm just speeding up your learning curves a little." Her eyes took on a faraway look. "You know what would really just float my boat? If you actually made the finals, and Allison Gaylord didn't."

"Her speech was okay," Dawn said. " 'Appreciating Senior Citizens.' She just oozed sincerity. I suppose the judges like that, right?"

"I'm not talking about her speech—" Scarlett started to say but was interrupted by a couple of knocks on the door. She walked over, looked through the peephole, and then opened it for Katie and Gigi.

"We're ten minutes early, sorry," Gigi said. "But this'll give us a chance to dish."

"We were just talking about this afternoon's platform rehearsals," Scarlett-Caress told them.

"Could you believe Allison Gaylord?" Gigi wanted to know.

"What about her?" Dawn asked. "Scarlett-Caress was just saying the same thing."

"Nothing she did would surprise me, after what she said

to me at Wave Country," Katie said. "She pretty much called me a fat pig to my face."

"She's just trying to psych you out," Scarlett-Caress explained. "It's her usual thing. She susses out a girl's weakness and goes after it until that girl is totally demoralized. Demoralized girls don't win beauty pageants."

"Well, this afternoon The Virus pulled a real beaut," Gigi said. "She was out there in the audience, and when everyone applauded at the end of a person's speech—"

"She clapped her hands together, but did it so they didn't actually touch—" Scarlett-Caress put in.

"Exactly, so she didn't make any sound!" Gigi finished. "Now, how nasty is that?"

"I'm telling you, she's The Virus," Scarlett-Caress insisted. "She's absolutely deadly."

"We should just ignore her," Katie suggested.

"That would be like ignoring the bubonic plague." Scarlett-Caress turned to Katie. "I might as well tell you, Katie, I truly get the feeling Allison Gaylord doesn't like you at all."

"I get that feeling, too," Katie admitted. "I have no idea why she's zeroing in on me. I've never done anything to her!"

"That doesn't matter," Scarlett-Caress replied. "At every pageant, she picks a victim. The victim is always an outsider who she thinks has an actual shot at winning." She paused. "And at this particular pageant, I think you're it."

CHAPTER

9

"Hey, how's my girl?" Trey's voice purred through the phone into Gigi's ear.

"Lonely for you," Gigi replied, staring up at the ceiling as she lay on her bed in her hotel room. "My roommate is downstairs somewhere rehearsing on her violin, so we can talk as dirty as we want," she added.

Trey laughed. "Is that so? Why don't you tell me what you've been doing there for the last few days first?"

Gigi rolled over on to her stomach, idly swinging her legs in the air. "I can't believe we start our second week tomorrow. They keep us so busy that before one day ends, it feels like the next day begins."

"Has anyone heard you sing yet?"

"Only the musical coordinator, this guy named Dean Paisley," Gigi said. "He said I knocked his socks off."

"As long as you don't knock his drawers off," Trey teased her.

"You know the only one I want is you."

"Right back at ya, Geeg."

"How's your tour?"

"It's great," Trey said. "Marie got vocal nodes, so we picked up a new backup singer named Cassandra. Now, this girl can *sing!*"

Even though Gigi knew it was silly, she instantly felt jealous. "Is she better than me?"

"Different," Trey replied.

Gigi sat up. "You weren't supposed to say that. You were supposed to say, 'She can't shine your red platform shoes, Gigi.'"

"You jealous?" Trey teased.

"Is she cute?"

"Who, Cassandra?"

"No, your mama. *Of course* Cassandra!" Gigi snapped.

"She's all right," Trey said carefully. "I mean, backup singers are always good-looking. It's part of the gig."

"She *is* cute," Gigi said, dread filling her heart. "You know, Trey, I was thinking. About when you get to Memphis . . ."

"Yeah?"

"Well, how could we be so close to each other and not be together? Especially when my parents are far, far away?"

"What about the pageant rules?"

"What about them?"

"You know I want to be with you, baby," Trey said, "but I don't want to get you kicked out of the pageant. Unless you've come to your senses and realized it's a white-girl thing, that is."

Gigi decided to ignore that last comment. She wasn't about to get into a fight with Trey about racism. "Trey, I really, really want you to come and visit me," she said softly. "I won't get caught. When can you be here?"

"Friday," Trey said. "We have one dark night."

"Call me when you get here. If I don't answer, leave me a message and I'll call you at your hotel."

"I guess I shouldn't stay at *your* hotel, huh?"

"Not a chance," Gigi replied. "I'm going to find a way to sneak out and be with you."

"Are you sure you want to risk—"

"I'm sure," Gigi said. "Just think, Trey. We'll be alone. I mean *really* alone. In a hotel. For the very first time."

"I don't think I'll be able to sleep between now and then," Trey confessed.

"Me, either," Gigi said. "I love you, Trey. And the night after tomorrow night, I'm going to prove it to you."

"Well, girls, here we are at the beginning of week number two," Mrs. Crownwell-Stevens said into the microphone. "I think you should all give yourself a round of applause for the wonderful job you've been doing."

All the contestants, assembled in the ballroom Sunday morning after breakfast, clapped enthusiastically.

"Today, our judges begin a more serious, in-depth evaluation of each of you. If you'll refer to your schedule for the next two days, you'll see that all of you are scheduled for private thirty-minute interviews with the judges. You will rehearse both your evening-gown presentation number and your physical-fitness number with Jimmy, and more choreography and blocking rehearsal will follow your dinner with the Nashville Jaycees this evening.

"Tomorrow night, of course, is our first round in the talent competition. Each of you who is performing with the orchestra is scheduled for a rehearsal with them sometime today. Please check the master schedule. Please be prompt."

A nervous hum went through the room. The following evening would be the first time that they would see each other perform, and, much more importantly, that the judges would evaluate their performances. Only the top twelve girls, the regional semifinalists, would actually perform on the last night of the pageant.

"As you know, rehearsal space here at the hotel is available whenever you are not otherwise scheduled. Remember to sign up for rehearsal time with Dean on the master list in the Teen Spirit suite on the penthouse level of the hotel. Also, today and tomorrow we'll provide two other rehearsal pianists, or you can work with your own prerecorded music."

Mrs. Crownwell-Stevens took a sip of water from the glass on the podium, then she smiled at them. "In my experience with pageants, this is the day that you all start to get really, really nervous."

A few chuckles of agreement rippled through the air.

"I can only assure you that you are all here because you are wonderful, special young women. Miss Teen Spirit isn't just about winning. It's about standing tall and being who you are. Thank you, and have a wonderful day."

They applauded again and the group broke up as girls headed out of the ballroom. Scarlett-Caress walked out with Dawn. "If it isn't about winning, then I ask you, why do they pick a national Miss Teen Spirit?"

"And why don't the regional losers get the same five thousand dollars as the regional winners?" Dawn asked as they approached the door.

"Y'all, I am so nervous I'm about to wet my pants," Shyanne confessed, catching up with them. "I have the very first private interview with the judges this morning."

"Just be your charming little self," Scarlett-Caress suggested.

"Oh, I know that," Shyanne assured them as they walked toward the lobby. "But the judges can ask anything. Take current events. I study the newspapers every night until I'm so tired I feel like I've been rode hard and put up wet. But when I get nervous, it all just flies out of my head! What time is your private interview?"

"Three this afternoon," Scarlett-Caress said.

"Mine's in an hour," Dawn said.

"You must be nervous, too, then," Shyanne said. "Oh, golly!" She stood stock-still.

"What?" Dawn asked.

"I just forgot the name of one of the justices on the Supreme Court! Scalia, Thomas, Ginsberg—"

"You memorized the names of the entire Supreme Court?" Dawn was incredulous.

"Uh-huh." Shyanne nodded proudly. "You never know what they'll ask. I also memorized the presidents and vice-presidents, in order." She looked around the crowded lobby. "I have to find Beth. She'll know which justice I forgot. See y'all!"

Dawn looked up at Scarlett-Caress. "The judges don't really ask you stuff like that . . . do they?"

Scarlett-Caress shrugged. "If they're in a perverse mood, they might. But as long as you're reasonably articulate and incredibly precious when you tell them you don't know the answer, they couldn't care less."

She yawned and looked at her watch. "I'm rehearsing with the orchestra in an hour. I hate getting stuck with morning talent rehearsal. Who can sing before noon?"

They stood in a huge crowd of girls, waiting for the elevator to show up. The two other elevators had signs on them that said OUT OF ORDER.

"When did you say your interview was?" Scarlett-Caress asked.

"In an hour."

"And you'll be wearing . . . ?"

"I was thinking totally nude," Dawn deadpanned.

"And *I* was thinking that ice-blue suit with the short skirt I saw hanging in the closet," Scarlett-Caress said sweetly. "I've got a lacy camisole you can wear under the jacket. It'll give you a demure but slightly sexy look."

"Yeah, I guess nude would look better on Wanda Sue, anyway," Dawn said as Wanda Sue walked by in a tiny cropped T-shirt and minuscule skirt.

"Oh, sugar." Scarlett-Caress snapped her fingers. "I left my sheet music in the ballroom. I'll see you upstairs, roomie," she added, hurrying off.

Katie had to dodge around her as she walked over to Dawn. "How's it going?"

Dawn shrugged. "It's going."

"Meaning you're not . . . doing what you said you might do?" Katie didn't want to say it out loud since they were surrounded by other girls.

"Not this minute," Dawn said. "I could change my mind during the endless choreography rehearsals today, though. I really, really detest Delancy."

"He's not exactly a sensitive person," Katie agreed. "Uh-oh," she added, looking over her shoulder. "Look who's headed our way."

"Good morning!" Allison called chirpily as she bounced over to them. "Isn't it a lovely day?"

"How would we know, we're in the hotel the entire day," Dawn said.

"Oh, silly-billy." Allison hit Dawn playfully on the arm. "You just need to have a more upbeat attitude!"

Dawn looked to her right and then to her left. "I'm a little confused here, Allison. Why are you in your disgustingly sweet mode instead of your monster-from-hell mode? There aren't any judges around."

As if on cue, Molly Cantor pushed through the crowd of

girls to ring for the elevator again. She'd been behind Dawn, so Dawn hadn't seen her.

"These elevators take forever," Mrs. Cantor groused. "I was supposed to be at a meeting upstairs five minutes ago."

"Good morning, Mrs. Cantor!" Allison sang. "Would you like me to see if there's a private elevator or a freight elevator you could use?"

"No thanks, honey," Mrs. Cantor said. "But I certainly will be complaining to the management about this."

Finally the elevator arrived, and girls streamed into it quickly until it was packed.

"Y'all, could a couple of you please wait and let Mrs. Cantor get on?" Allison called to them. "She's late for a meeting."

Instantly all the girls streamed back out of the elevator, chagrined to have missed seeing a judge in their midst. None of them wanted to be the one who hadn't given up her place for Mrs. Cantor.

The judge laughed. "I'm not that huge, girls. A few of you really can fit into the elevator with me. Allison?"

"Oh, thanks so much, but I'll wait," Allison said. "Dawn's chair takes up quite a bit of space, and I'm kind of taking care of her. We wouldn't want to put out so many of the other girls, would we, Dawn?"

Dawn was so angry that she couldn't even speak.

"You are just the sweetest," Mrs. Cantor said, stepping into the elevator. None of the other girls were sure if they should get on or not. Finally, Beth and Michelle stepped in, then others followed.

When the elevator doors closed, Dawn turned to Allison, her face red with fury. "Don't you ever, *ever* use me like that again, or I will make sure you are humiliated in front of every judge at the pageant."

"I'm just *trembling* with worry over that," Allison said

sarcastically. She fixed her gaze on Katie. "Just a little tip, honey. If you continue to pack on the pounds like you have been, they're gonna have to reinforce the stage during the opening dance number."

Even though Katie had vowed to herself that she wouldn't rise to Allison's bait, she found herself protesting, "I haven't gained any weight!"

Allison chuckled. "Honey, one of the judges wrote 'heifer' on your pageant form. I saw it with my own two eyes!"

Willow, who had overheard Allison's remarks, sauntered over to them. "Allison, I'm curious. Do you actually enjoy being so nasty?"

Allison shrugged. "If a girl can't take some constructive criticism, then she shouldn't be here."

"Constructive criticism can be very helpful," Willow agreed. "That's why I'm certain you'll take what I'm about to say gracefully. You are a mean, petty, vindictive, nasty, rather ugly person, Allison. And if you think that winning this pageant is worth being all that, then I feel rather sorry for you."

A small group of girls who had overheard applauded.

Allison tossed her hair off her shoulders with an I-could-care-less attitude, but her face told the truth. It was bright red.

"I guess you think yours doesn't stink, Willow," she said. "Well, think again. I haven't met a girl at a pageant yet who didn't have a skeleton in her closet. I intend to find out yours."

Nothing showed on Willow's beautiful face as she replied, "I have nothing to hide."

"Oh, really?" Allison asked coolly. "Well, we'll see about that, Miss Perfect." Her eyes narrowed to angry, cold slits. "Katie-the-Cow isn't really worth my time. I think I'm going to ruin you, instead."

She smiled malevolently. "And there's not a thing in the world that you can do about it."

"Dawn, it's a pleasure to see you again," Dr. Franklin, one of the judges, said as Dawn entered the interview room.

All the judges were sitting at a long table, with pens, notebooks, and crystal goblets of water in front of them. They smiled at Dawn as she wheeled herself over to them.

She had indeed worn her ice-blue suit with Scarlett-Caress's white camisole. She had refused to wear a matching blue ribbon in her hair, even though her roommate insisted that for some reason male judges went crazy for hair ribbons. She did let Scarlett-Caress talk her out of wearing her favorite shoes—Nubuck blue loafers scattered with white stars (*way* too trendy, Scarlett-Caress had decreed). Instead she wore demure white pumps, compliments of Scarlett-Caress.

They're two sizes too big on me, Dawn thought nervously as she wheeled over to the judges, *but, hey, I can't walk, so it's not like they'll fall off!*

Her heart was pounding. She had spoken to all the judges many times, but this was her first official private thirty-minute interview. There would be one more later in the week. The score in these two interviews played a big part in winning the pageant.

The night before, Scarlett-Caress had spent two hours coaching Dawn for her interview. In spite of all her ambivalence about the pageant, her competitive spirit had gotten the best of her, and she'd soaked up her roommate's advice.

"They want to pick a girl they like," Scarlett-Caress had

said. "And they'll decide if they like you in the first long interview, so listen carefully.

"Remember to smile at the judges when you enter the room. They're supposed to make you feel comfortable. But really it's *your* job to make *them* feel comfortable, and then they'll end up thinking *they're* the ones who made *you* feel comfortable, and then they'll like you. Simple!"

Dawn smiled at the judges. Her mouth was bone-dry. Her teeth were sticking to her lips.

"Well, Dawn, how has the first week gone for you?" Connie Restry asked warmly. She was an executive with Polimar Records in Nashville.

"Just great," Dawn said in her best pageant voice. "All the girls are really terrific."

All the judges smiled and nodded.

"Has it been difficult for you, being the only physically challenged girl in the pageant?" Dr. Franklin asked.

"They'll undoubtedly hit the physically challenged thing big time," Scarlett-Caress had said. "It's your strong suit, so play it for all it's worth. You are brave and spunky and inspirational at all times. And the other girls are just wonderful, every single one of them."

"Oh, no," Dawn replied instantly. "All the girls have been so helpful to me. You know, all those people who think badly of today's teens should see the wonderful girls at this pageant. I know it would change their minds."

The judges smiled at her again, and jotted something down. Dawn kept smiling. She sat up straight, both hands demurely in her lap, one hand on top of the other, per Scarlett-Caress's instructions.

"As a physically challenged teen, what would it mean to you to be chosen Miss Teen Spirit?" Molly Cantor asked.

"Miss Teen Spirit is every girl," Dawn said, "but she's the highest sense of every girl. If I'm fortunate enough to be chosen Miss Teen Spirit, it will send a message to every girl out there that there need not be any limitations to her dreams."

The interview continued. Dawn was able to answer every question easily. They asked her more about Helping Hands, and what it meant to her. One judge asked her about a recent Supreme Court ruling—thankfully they didn't ask her to name the justices themselves—and she was able to keep her answer short, intelligent, and articulate without actually saying anything that could be construed as controversial, just as Scarlett-Caress had tutored her.

Everything went wonderfully well, and it was clear to Dawn by the end of the half hour that the judges both admired and liked her.

The only problem was that the girl the judges liked was nothing like the real Dawn Faison. Instead, she was a wheelchair-bound version of her roommate. Not only was she wearing Scarlett-Caress's shoes, she was wearing Scarlett-Caress's personality.

As Dawn wheeled herself back to the elevator she felt kind of nauseous, and it took her a minute to realize what was making her feel that way.

Then, it finally dawned on her.

So what if the interview went great and the judges loved me? she asked herself. *I have just become exactly what I loathe: a pageant-head.*

Katie was breathing hard as she attempted her double front tuck on the trampoline again. It was her best trick, but in the past forty-five minutes of rehearsing her routine, she hadn't hit it once.

"Just concentrate," she coached herself out loud, jumping

lightly on the small, portable trampoline that had been rented for her. "You can do this."

She didn't want to get off the trampoline to turn her taped music back on, so she hummed it softly as she went into the last part of her routine. Jump, jump higher, and higher, head down, tuck and tuck and . . .

Boom. Once again she had overrotated and landed on her butt.

"Sitting down on the job?"

Katie looked up. Dean Paisley was standing in the doorway of her rehearsal room.

"I might as well," Katie said ruefully. "I sit on this thing a lot better than I do the acrobatics I'm supposed to be doing."

Dean walked into the room. "Can I watch?"

"No, you can't watch," Katie told him, wiping the sweat off her forehead. She pulled down the sides of her gym shorts. "I feel self-conscious enough when *nobody* is watching. Besides, aren't you supposed to be rehearsing with someone or other who actually has some talent?"

"Now, see, you have to stop downing yourself like that," Dean said, lazily leaning his elbows on the trampoline. "You look mighty cute up there, I might add."

"Really, Dean, I don't think you're supposed to be in here—"

"I'm on a break."

"I mean I don't think we're supposed to be alone," Katie said nervously.

"You're right," Dean admitted. "When a guy like me is as attracted as I am to a girl like you, you never know what could happen if this guy and girl were alone. . . ."

Katie tried not to look at his sexy lips. "Be serious. I don't want to get kicked out of the pageant, and neither do you."

"Okay, okay," Dean said. "I'll leave on one condition."

"What?"

He reached out and barely touched the edge of Katie's gym shorts. An electric thrill ran up her leg. "If you let me see just one trick. Come on, I'll be a great audience. It'll help your confidence."

Katie stood up. "If that's what it takes to get you to leave—"

"Meaning you don't want to be alone with me?" Dean asked.

"I . . . I can't think about you now," Katie stammered, not looking at him.

"Funny, I can't stop thinking about you," Dean said. "After the pageant is over, I was thinking—"

"That I'll be back in Virginia," Katie interrupted. "And you'll be in Chicago at the Miss Midwest Teen Spirit pageant."

"I wouldn't let geography stop us," Dean said. "Would you?"

Katie stared at her hands. "I don't know," she finally whispered.

Dean smiled. "I didn't mean to put you on the spot, Katie, honest. How about if you show me that trick, I applaud wildly, and we'll table this conversation until after you get picked as a finalist."

"Fat chance," Katie muttered, jumping lightly on the trampoline. "Okay, here's my trick, which I haven't landed all day. Wish me luck."

"Good luck!"

Katie bounced higher and higher.

Maybe the problem is that I haven't been getting enough height before I tuck, she thought, and bounced higher still. Then she tucked her head in, and used the force of the motion to propel herself over, and, yes, she was going to be able to time the second rotation. She almost had it, almost—

When her ankle made sudden, sharp contact with the side of the trampoline. Instinctively she tried to right herself, and felt her ankle turn inward at a sickening angle. She fell onto her back, grabbing her ankle, tears of pain filling her eyes.

"Katie! God, what happened?" Dean asked as he scrambled onto the trampoline to help her.

"My ankle hit the brace of the trampoline," Katie said as tears coursed down her cheeks. "Then it twisted funny . . . it really hurts."

"Do you think you can walk?" Dean asked.

"How could I be so stupid?" Katie berated herself. "I wasn't even centered on the trampoline, I jumped too high—"

"This is no time to beat yourself up." Dean reached for her. "Let me help you down from there."

He lifted Katie in his strong arms and gently carried her down to the floor. She stood, all her weight resting on her left foot, her injured foot in the air. Dean kept his arms around her to steady her.

"We need to call the hotel doctor," he said.

"No, no, maybe I can walk it off."

"But what if you broke it? What if walking on it injures it even more?"

"Let me just try," Katie insisted.

"Look, if you can't walk, then you obviously can't—"

"You don't understand," Katie cried. "You don't know anything about me, or how much this pageant means to me. Don't you see? If I miss the talent competition, I'm out! I've come so far, I can't give it all up without a fight. I won't!"

Dean sighed. "Okay. But I'm not letting go of you. Just slowly put your right foot down. Just try a little weight."

Katie gingerly put her right foot on the ground. Her ankle was throbbing with pain, but she refused to feel it. Little by little, she put some weight on it.

"Okay?" Dean asked, still holding her.

"Let go of me," Katie said. "Please. I have to see if I can do this."

Reluctantly, Dean dropped his arms.

I can do this, she told herself. *I can take a step. And then another. And another. I can do this!*

Her heart in her mouth, Katie stepped on to her right foot.

And collapsed to the floor from the excruciating pain.

"No, no, this can't be happening to me!" she sobbed.

Dean lifted her, and held her in his arms. "Shhhh. Let me get you to a doctor, Katie—"

At that moment, with Katie cradled in Dean's arms, Mrs. Drummond, the strictest chaperon in the pageant, appeared in the doorway. She took in the two of them, Katie in Dean's arms, and her jaw dropped open.

"This is appalling!" she said, dramatically clapping her hands to her bosom. "Just what in God's name do the two of you think you're doing?"

CHAPTER

10

Katie sat on the edge of her bed, twisting a tissue between her fingers over and over. Her eyes were so red and swollen from crying that she could barely see.

After all her hard work, her hopes and dreams, was it really over? Gone was the chance, however slim it might have been, to be one of the six winners chosen to go on to the national Miss Teen Spirit Pageant. There would be no money, no fame, and worst of all, no college scholarship.

Katie thought back on the last few hours, which had been the worst hours of her entire life. The hotel doctor had taken one look at her ankle and ordered her to Baptist Hospital for X rays. Dean had wanted to go with her, but Katie was sure that doing so would only make both of them look even more guilty than they already looked. Besides, he had rehearsals scheduled all day. In the end one of the nicer chaperons accompanied her in a hotel limousine.

The X rays had shown that Katie's ankle was badly sprained—the bruising was already ugly. The doctor at Baptist had acted as if she expected Katie to be happy that it wasn't broken. But what difference did it make? She

couldn't possibly perform in the talent competition the next
night with a sprained ankle, because there was no way she
could jump on the trampoline. She couldn't even be in the
opening dance number, because she was walking around on
crutches.

And even all of *that* didn't really matter, because Mrs.
Drummond had reported her and Dean for severe rule
violations, violations serious enough to get Dean fired and
her thrown out of the pageant in disgrace.

When she'd returned from the hospital, a message had
been waiting for her in her room to call Mrs. Crownwell-
Stevens at once. When she did as she was asked, the pageant
director ordered her to report immediately to the hospitality
suite to discuss the charges that had been leveled against
her.

Willow had graciously offered to help Katie get up to the
suite, but Katie had insisted on going alone. When she
hobbled in on her crutches, Dean, Mrs. Drummond, and
Mrs. Crownwell-Stevens were already waiting there for her.

"Katie, have a seat," Mrs. Crownwell-Stevens said.

Dean rose and gently helped Katie into a chair.

"Thank you for coming, Katie. I'm very sorry about your
accident," Mrs. Crownwell-Stevens began.

"Thank you."

"Well, I'm afraid we have quite an ugly situation here,"
the woman continued. "Mrs. Drummond has reported that
the two of you have committed some very serious violations
of our pageant rules. Frankly, I have to say I'm both
surprised and disappointed. I expected more from both of
you."

"With all due respect, Mrs. Drummond, do you plan to
decide we're guilty before you even hear our side of the
story?" Dean asked.

"Young man, I know what I saw," Mrs. Drummond said self-righteously.

"Yes, I'm sure you do, Mrs. Drummond," Mrs. Crownwell-Stevens agreed. "But I'm sure you'll also agree that we owe it to these two young people to hear their side of things."

Mrs. Drummond huffed her disapproval, but clearly Mrs. Crownwell-Stevens was the boss.

"The most important thing that you need to know," Dean began, "is that Katie did absolutely nothing wrong. I had a break between rehearsals and I stopped into the room where she was practicing her trampoline routine. She didn't invite me. She didn't know I was coming. In fact, she asked me to leave."

"Is that true?" Mrs. Crownwell-Stevens asked Katie.

Katie thought a moment. *What should I do? Jane always tells me that I'm honest to a fault. Should I be completely honest now?*

"It's partly true," Katie said softly. "I didn't invite Dean to my rehearsal. I did ask him to leave. But I also agreed to let him watch one of my tricks on the trampoline before he left. And that's when I sprained my ankle."

"You were in his arms, young lady," Mrs. Drummond accused.

"She tried to walk on her injured ankle and she fell," Dean said. "Should I have left her there, Mrs. Drummond? Just so I wouldn't break one of your precious rules?"

"Katie?" Mrs. Crownwell-Stevens asked. "Can you cor-roborate that?"

Katie nodded. "I was determined to try to walk. I . . . I couldn't bear the thought of being forced to drop out of the pageant. It means so much to me. So I tried to put weight on my right foot, and I fell. And then Dean helped me up—"

"And then Mrs. Drummond walked in and hyperventi-lated before we could even begin to explain," Dean finished.

"Mrs. Drummond was just doing her job," Mrs. Crownwell-Stevens said. "I'm very grateful to her."

"I should think so!" the older woman exclaimed, only somewhat mollified by these words.

"However, Mrs. Crownwell-Stevens continued, "in light of this new information, I'll have to give this matter some serious thought before I made a decision. There are still some very grave rule violations here. And, I might add, Mr. Paisley, that you seem to have something of an attitude problem."

"I apologize for that, ma'am," Dean said. "I just don't like to be judged and found guilty before the trial. And one last thing. I'd like to stay with the pageant, but I'll accept whatever you decide about me. Don't take it out on Katie, though, when I'm the one who broke the rules."

Mrs. Crownwell-Stevens nodded thoughtfully. "I'll take all of this into consideration. I'll call your rooms with my decision within the next hour."

Clearly, it was a dismissal. Both Dean and Katie rose from their seats. Dean handed Katie her crutches.

"I'm going to make sure Katie gets to her room okay," he said, helping her to the door.

"Mr. Paisley, haven't you learned anything from this unfortunate episode?" Mrs. Drummond demanded icily.

Sensing a renewal of hostilities in the making, Mrs. Crownwell-Stevens quickly interceded. "As these are extenuating circumstances, that will be fine," she announced smoothly. "Thank you, Dean, for helping Katie to her room."

Katie looked at the clock on the nightstand for the zillionth time in the past hour and fifteen minutes.

Why hasn't she called yet? she wondered, still twisting the tissue in her hands nervously. She stared at the phone, willing it to ring, but it remained ominously silent.

"Can I get you anything?" Willow asked kindly. "A soft drink? Some water?"

"Nothing," Katie replied.

Willow's sympathy for her roommate was obvious. Katie had told her everything that had happened with Dean. Willow had come to really like Katie, and she desperately wished she could find a way to help her.

"Maybe she won't kick you out," she offered. "That would be awfully harsh."

"Rules are rules," Katie said. Tears filled her eyes again. "I can't believe this is happening to me!"

At that moment the phone rang. Katie snatched it up.

"Hello?"

"Katie? It's Mom."

It was the first time Katie's mother had called her during the pageant. Two days before Katie had left home, their phone had been turned off because the bill hadn't been paid. Katie's mother had assured her that she'd be able to turn the phone back on when she received her next paycheck, but every time Katie had dialed home, she'd gotten the recording about how the phone had been temporarily disconnected.

"Hi, Mom," Katie said, trying to sound upbeat. *Please don't let anything show in my voice,* she prayed. "So, I guess you got the phone turned back on, huh?"

"No, sugar, I'm calling from Jane's apartment."

"Didn't you get my letter?" Katie asked. "I told you to use some of my pageant money to take care of the phone problem."

Her mother didn't answer her question. "So, sugar, how is everything there?"

Katie swallowed hard. "Just great, Mom."

"I'm so glad."

"How's Daddy?"

"Well, that's what I was calling you about, sugar. I don't want you to fret about this, but your daddy had to go back into the hospital."

Katie felt her stomach churn. "But he was doing so well!"

"He was, sugar," her mother agreed. "But you know how he is, he just goes to a bad place in his head. I found him hiding in the bushes in front of the trailer, with his old shotgun. He was crouched in the bushes, waiting for the Viet Cong to attack. . . ."

"Oh, Mom . . ."

"Like I said, sugar, I wouldn't have even burdened you with this now, but it means your dad won't be going back to do that housepainting job your uncle Keiler fixed up for him. And the bills are all piled up. So if you could see fit to loan your mom just a couple hundred dollars of your pageant money, I'll pay it all back."

How many times have I heard that? Katie thought. *Almost every penny I ever made—baby-sitting, tutoring, mowing lawns, cleaning rich people's houses on the weekends, almost every penny has gone to my mom. Always broke. Always behind. Always in some kind of trouble.*

Always looking to Katie to come to the rescue.

And every single time she says she'll pay me back, but she never does.

She closed her eyes. She was so tired. What difference did it make anymore? Her dream of a college scholarship was finished. And the remaining fifteen hundred dollars she had from winning the Virginia pageant wasn't really going to change her life.

"Take as much money as you need, Mom," Katie said.

"Jane has my bankbook. She can withdraw money for you with her signature."

"Bless you, sweetheart," her mother said. "And remember now, this is only a loan. Until I can get us on our feet."

"Sure, Mom."

"Here, Jane wants to speak with you."

"Katie?"

Jane's warm and wonderful voice made Katie want to cry all over again.

"Hi," Katie managed.

"You sound terrible!"

"It's just . . . stress," Katie lied. "I'm fine."

"Listen, I told your mom I could lend her a couple hundred dollars—"

"You know she'll never be able to pay you back, Jane."

"Well, that's neither here nor there," Jane said, "because she turned me down. She said it was a family matter."

"That sounds like her."

"So, what do you want me to do?" Jane asked.

"Give her whatever she needs."

"Katie, are you sure?"

"I'm sure. Listen, Jane, I have to go to rehearsal. But I'll call you tomorrow, okay?"

"Collect," Jane insisted. "Are you sure you're okay?"

"I'm fine, really."

"Just remember, Katie, how proud I am of you. I'll be there at the pageant rooting for you like crazy next Sunday!"

Katie hung up, hobbled over to the bed, and threw herself on it. "I was stupid to think I could change my life," she sobbed.

"No—" Willow began.

"Yes! Girls like me don't win beauty pageants."

"That's not true," Willow insisted. Although she had

overheard only Katie's side of the conversation, some things had become clear to her. Katie was poor. Really poor.

Willow had had no idea.

"Well, now you know about me," Katie said, sitting up to grab another tissue from the box on the nightstand. She blew her nose. "My dad's crazy. He's been in and out of mental hospitals my whole life. My mom spends every penny she has playing Lotto so she can become a millionaire.

"Lots of the time our phone is turned off," she continued, determined to pour out the whole ugly story. "Or we don't have any electricity because my mom didn't pay the electric bill. We live in a trailer park. I work weekends cleaning the houses of rich girls like you."

She paused to blow her nose again. "I suppose you never even met a girl like me before. Unless she was doing your laundry or something."

"That's true," Willow agreed.

"I knew it," Katie said bitterly, terribly embarrassed.

"What I mean is, I never met anyone quite as terrific as you are, Katie."

"Please don't pull a be-nice-to-the-poor-girl on me."

Willow shook her head no. "I would never do that to you."

Katie looked into her roommate's eyes, and found that she believed her. "You're actually telling me the truth," she realized.

"I am," Willow said. "Whatever happens with the pageant, Katie, I hope . . . well, I don't actually have many close girlfriends. Actually, believe it or not, I don't have *any* close girlfriends. And it would mean so much to me if we could be . . ."

Katie laughed through her tears. "Bestest friends?"

Willow laughed. "Something like that. What do you think?"

"As long as we don't have to cut ourselves and bleed on each other to seal it like we did in third grade," Katie said.

"Deal," Willow agreed.

"Deal."

The phone rang again, the shrillness of it startling them both.

"This is it," Katie said. She took a deep breath to steady her nerves as Willow held up crossed fingers for luck.

Katie picked up the phone. "Hello?"

"Yes, Katie. Mrs. Crownwell-Stevens here."

"Yes."

"After giving this matter a great deal of thought, Katie, I've decided not to eliminate you from competing in the pageant."

Katie wasn't sure she had heard correctly. "You . . . you aren't kicking me out?"

"No," Mrs. Crownwell-Stevens replied. "I believe you showed poor judgment in not demanding that Mr. Paisley leave your rehearsal immediately, but I also believe this was not some preplanned clandestine meeting between the two of you."

"No, no, it wasn't," Katie said eagerly, her heart soaring with hope.

"What is she saying?" Willow whispered.

Katie beamed at her roommate and gave her a thumbs-up sign even as she listened intently to every word the pageant director was saying.

"As for Mr. Paisley, he is an employee rather than a contestant, though I've told him that if he violates one of our rules again, I'll be forced to let him go. Other than that, this incident will remain between the three of us. And Mrs. Drummond, of course."

Katie could feel the relief coursing through her body. " I

can't thank you enough, Mrs. Crownwell-Stevens. I'm
just . . . I'm so happy."

"You're a wonderful young woman, Katie," Mrs.
Crownwell-Stevens said warmly. "You're a credit to our
pageant. I know this type of thing will never happen again."

"No, no, never!" Katie cried. "I promise!"

"Your word is good enough for me," Mrs. Crownwell-
Stevens said. "There is something else we need to address,
though. Your sprained ankle is going to put something of a
dent in your ability to compete."

"I know," Katie said. "I won't be able to dance, or do the
physical-fitness competition, or do my talent."

"It's the talent that concerns me," Mrs. Crownwell-
Stevens said. "I'm afraid I don't see any way around that,
unless you're secretly an amazing singer and you've never
mentioned it."

"I can barely carry a tune," Katie admitted.

"Well, at least you'll be in the pageant," Mrs. Crownwell-
Stevens concluded. "That's something, isn't it?"

"What if I could think of a new talent?" Katie asked.
"Something that I could actually do with a sprained ankle?"

"If you think of it, I promise to be open-minded."

"Thank you," Katie said. "For everything." She hung up
the phone.

"I'm still in!" she screamed, throwing her arms around
Willow.

Willow hugged her back. "I'm so happy for you! We
should celebrate. I know what we need—champagne!"

"Ha-ha," Katie said, pretending that Willow had only
been joking.

"No, I'm serious," Willow said. "I actually have a little
bottle in one of my suitcases." She got off the bed and
headed for the closet where her suitcases were stashed.

"Willow," Katie said slowly, "I almost got kicked out of

the pageant for breaking a rule. Where did you get that bottle?"

Willow laughed. "My uncle is this big liquor distributor back in New Orleans."

"If we got caught drinking . . ."

Willow laughed again. "Oh, who's going to catch us?"

"A chaperon, maybe?" Katie watched as her roommate rummaged through the closet. "Willow, really. I don't want any."

"Are you sure?"

"Positive." Katie hesitated. "So . . . do you drink a lot?"

"Yes," Willow said dramatically, her voice teasing. "I'm secretly a great big lush. You've found me out!"

Katie laughed and went along with the joke, but secretly she was worried that there might be some truth in what Willow had just told her.

But that's silly, she thought. *Every single girl here believes Willow is the girl to beat in this pageant. She couldn't possibly be so wonderful if she was really a teen alcoholic.*

"Willow, I hope this doesn't offend you, but . . ."

"What?"

"I know I'm just being paranoid because I almost got kicked out," Katie said, "but what if someone searches our room and finds your champagne?"

Willow put her hands on her slender hips. Her eyes danced with mirth. "Katie, you don't honestly believe they would search our rooms, do you?"

"They might. So could you humor me and make sure there's no liquor in here? Pretty-please-and-I'll-be-your-bestest-friend?"

Willow rolled her eyes. "Oh, all right. For you. There's

only the one tiny bottle anyway. Any other requests, Ms. Laramie?"

"Yes," Katie said. "A big one."

Willow sat on her bed cross-legged. "What's that?"

"Find me a new talent. Something fantastic that doesn't involve walking, running, or dancing. And whatever it is, I have to become an expert at it by tomorrow night!"

"How about a speech?" Gigi suggested.

"She's already giving a platform speech," Beth pointed out as she sat on the floor doing biceps curls with her dumbbells. "It would be redundant."

"You could tell jokes," Shyanne offered. "As long as they were clean, of course."

"I'm terrible at telling jokes," Katie said. "I can never remember the punch lines."

News about Katie's accident had spread through the pageant like wildfire, and after dinner, a spontaneous meeting had been convened to help her find a new talent. Now it was past ten o'clock at night, and the five girls who remained with Katie and Willow in their room—Gigi, Dawn, Scarlett-Caress, Beth, and Shyanne—had been brainstorming for over an hour . . . without managing to come up with a single viable idea.

"What if you read poetry?" Dawn suggested.

"Nah," they all replied at the same time.

"Oh, oh, wait, y'all, I've got it!" Shyanne exclaimed, rising to her knees on the bed. "You can do Joan of Arc! You know that 'your counsel is of the devil. But mine is of God' speech? That would be inspirational!"

"Don't know it, can't act." Katie sighed with frustration. "The problem is, I don't have any talent!"

"Hey, now, you can't take a negative attitude about this," Shyanne chided her. "I read in the *Big Pageant Book*—the Bible of beauty pageants—that when it comes to talent, judges consider execution and skill, technical difficulty, confidence, discipline, and dedication—"

"What did you do, memorize the list?" Gigi asked.

"Oh, it wasn't hard. I have that kind of memory where you just remember everything you read. Except when I get nervous, and then—"

"Everything just flies out of your head," all the other girls chanted together, since they'd heard Shyanne say this so many times.

Dawn looked at Shyanne curiously. "What are you, a ringer?"

"What's a ringer?" Shyanne asked.

"Someone who deliberately leads everyone to underestimate them," Dawn explained. "And then that someone—surprise, surprise—ends up winning everything."

Shyanne laughed. "Oh, Lordy, no!"

"Oh, Lordy, yes," Beth corrected her. "Little ol' you happens to be a member of Brainiacs."

"Brainiacs? For teens with genius-level IQs?" Gigi asked. "Get out of town!"

Shyanne blushed. "It's not so hard to get in, I reckon."

"Shyanne, you have to have an IQ over one forty," Beth pointed out. "Since I'm a member, I keyed into the private register of members on my computer and cross-checked all the girls in this pageant. I knew Becky Haas was a member, of course, since she's here representing them. But I didn't know you were."

"I'm not the bragging type," Shyanne exclaimed.

Willow laughed. "I really want to be the one to drop this little tidbit to Allison. She treats you like you're slow-witted."

Shyanne smiled. "Well, now, that's her problem, isn't it?"

Dawn threw her head back and hooted. "This is too rich! She thinks she's psyching you out, and all the time you're psyching her out. I love it!"

"Y'all, I hate to spoil the party, but curfew is in forty-five minutes, and I still don't have a talent," Katie reminded them.

"The rules clearly state you can display a talent, give a speech, or demonstrate a hobby," Beth said. "What are your hobbies?"

Cleaning rich girls' houses so we can pay the rent, Katie thought. She and Willow traded looks, but neither said anything.

"I guess I don't have any," Katie admitted.

"Singing," Willow said firmly. "It's got to be singing. That's the only thing left."

"I'm telling you, I can *not* sing."

"Sugar dumpling, I think you're missing the point, here." Scarlett-Caress, silent up till now, spoke up. "Plenty of girls have sung in pageants with no more talent than a plucked chicken and still walked away with the crown. All you need to do is entertain the audience and look incredibly fetching while you do it."

"How can I when I haven't got any confidence?" Katie asked. "Believe me, I am the world's worst singer!"

"Good, sugar bunny, then you won't sing better than me," Scarlett-Caress said sweetly. "But since six girls are going to win this pageant, I can afford to be big about it. Now get up and give us a tune! And look fetching."

All the other girls joined in, urging Katie to get off the bed and sing.

"All right, all right." Katie stood up on her left foot. Willow handed her her crutches. "What should I sing?"

"Anything," Beth said. "This is merely a test."

"The only song I know all the words to is 'Happy Birthday,'" Katie confessed grumpily.

"So, sing it," Dawn said.

Katie put the crutches under her arms. "The answer to the question 'Katie, do you feel like an idiot right now?' is a big, fat *yes*." Reluctantly, she sang "Happy Birthday" as quickly as she could.

The room was silent.

"You were right," Gigi finally said. "You stink."

"I told you so!" Katie plopped back down on her bed, between Gigi and Beth. "Which leaves me exactly nowhere."

"Let's go through the alphabet for ideas," Shyanne suggested. "A . . . that could be archery. B . . . ballet? C . . . Candle making?"

"D . . . dumb idea," Gigi interjected.

"We need to go about this more scientifically," Beth decided as she recorded her biceps curls on her workout chart. "Think back on anything you were ever good at. Don't leave anything out. Free-associate. Let your mind wander."

"Let's see. I was a great hopscotch player in kindergarten," Katie began. "I won third place in a Thanksgiving draw-the-turkey contest when I was eight and won a free turkey."

"Keep going," Willow urged her.

"Uh . . . I can cross my eyes and make my tongue touch my nose at the same time," Katie said.

Everyone shook their heads vigorously.

Katie searched her mind frantically. "I used to do really stupid magic tricks with my best friend, Tiffany. I can hold my breath under water for—"

"Wait, wait, hold the phone!" Gigi yelled. "Go back to the magic tricks."

"What?" Katie asked.

"It's perfect!" Dawn agreed. "No one else is doing magic."

"Dawn, I was ten years old. The tricks were awful!"

"Honey buns, you are a desperate woman," Scarlett-Caress pointed out. "And desperate women resort to desperate measures. Besides, if you wear something flirty like a little leotard and top hat, and poor little ol' you is on your crutches, and all the judges know you were forced to change your talent at the last minute due to a horrible accident . . ." She let her words trail off.

"You know, I actually think it's a good idea," Willow told Katie.

"But I'm telling you, I don't know how to *do* magic," Katie protested. "Tiffany and I just had this dumb little book that taught you how to pretend a nickel was coming out of your ear or something. I would look like a total idiot!"

"Clearly, what you need is a really good book on magic," Beth said.

"And a really cute outfit," Scarlett-Caress added.

"Y'all, I cannot do magic," Katie began as the phone rang. She leaned over and picked it up. "Hello?"

"Katie? It's Dean."

"Oh, hi," she said softly.

"Is it a guy?" Gigi teased. "Because your voice just went to low and throaty big time!"

The other girls laughed and loudly teased Katie, who put a finger in her ear so she could block out the noise. "I'm

going to change phones, okay?" she asked Dean, careful not
to say to whom she was speaking.

"I'm taking it in the bathroom," Katie said, hopping on
her left foot. "Could you hang it up, Willow?"

"I knew there was some good reason that they had phones
in there!" Gigi called as Katie hopped into the bathroom.

Katie sat on the edge of the bathtub and picked up the
phone. "Dean? Are you okay?"

"I didn't get canned, if that's what you mean," he replied.
"I was more concerned about you. If what I did had gotten
you kicked out of the pageant, I never would have forgiven
myself."

"She didn't kick me out."

"I know," Dean said. "I wanted to apologize to you
anyway. I could have ruined everything for you—"

"It's okay, Dean, really."

"Somehow I knew you'd be nice about it. That's just the
kind of girl you are, Katie. So, how's your ankle?"

"It hurts," she admitted. "But that's not my big problem.
I might still be in the pageant, but I have no talent to do
tomorrow night. Which means that no matter what, I won't
be chosen to go on to nationals."

"And it's my fault," Dean said.

"You're not the one who messed up the trick, *I* am," Katie
told him firmly. She sighed and leaned her head against the
cool tile of the wall. "There's one good thing, though. A
whole bunch of girls are in my room right now, trying to
help me think up a new talent for tomorrow night."

"I'd have thought the other girls would be happy that
you're out of it," Dean said.

"Well, that's what I mean about a good thing. These girls
aren't like that. Don't you think that's great?"

"Frankly, Katie, I think you're great," Dean answered.
"So, what talents did you guys come up with?"

"None that count." She sighed again.

Through the bathroom door, Katie heard her friends begin to chant: "Magic! Magic! Magic! Magic!"

"What are they saying?" Dean asked.

"Y'all cut it out!" Katie called to them. It didn't diminish their chanting a bit. "They're chanting that I should do magic," she said, laughing. "I made the mistake of telling them I did these bad magic tricks when I was a kid, and—"

"That's it!" Dean cried.

"Not you, too." Katie groaned.

"No, you don't understand. All through high school I made money by doing magic at kids' parties," Dean said excitedly. "I'd play the piano and I'd do magic tricks. It was a huge hit!"

"I guess that means you can compete for the title of Miss Teen Spirit," Katie said.

"Very funny. Katie, I could teach you, I know I could."

"Aren't you forgetting something?" Katie asked. "Like that we'd both get instantly canned if we got caught?"

"So we won't get caught, then," Dean said. "Come on. Say yes."

"Dean, I can't—"

"You can!" he insisted.

"But if we got caught—"

"We'd get thrown out, you already said that," Dean said impatiently. "But if you don't do it, you know you'll lose. One way you risk failing, the other way you're certain of failing. Now, how about taking a risk, Miss Teen Spirit Virginia?"

Through the door Katie could hear her friends laughing and carrying on.

I know they care about me, she thought. *But in a week this whole thing will be over for all but six lucky girls. And tomorrow night all my friends will perform talents that*

*they've worked on for months, or even years. They've all
had lessons and coaches and special training that my
parents could never afford to give me. Mediocre trampoline
tricks were always a long shot, anyway.*

How much more of a long shot could mediocre magic be?

*And I want that college scholarship more than anything
in the world.*

"Dean?"

"I'm still here. Did you make a decision?"

"Yep," Katie said. "When do we start practicing?"

When Dawn and Scarlett-Caress arrived back at their room,
Scarlett-Caress jumped into the shower. Dawn quickly
dialed Kelly's number in Starkville. She had left three
messages on Kelly's machine, but her friend hadn't called
her back.

I can't believe I actually hung up on Kelly, Dawn
recalled, filled with guilt and remorse all over again. *I've
just got to get a hold of her so I can apologize.*

She couldn't understand why Kelly wasn't returning her
calls. Unless she was so angry that she didn't even want to
be Dawn's friend anymore.

But she wouldn't do that, Dawn thought anxiously as she
listened to Kelly's phone ringing. *We've been through too
much together.*

"Hi, this is Kelly, do what you need to do at the beep,"
came Kelly's voice on her answering machine.

"Kel? I hope you're getting my messages," Dawn said. "I
really, really need to talk to you. You can't stay mad at me
forever, can you? So just . . . call me, okay?" She hung up
the phone.

"The water pressure in the shower is on the fritz,"

Scarlett-Caress announced, emerging from the bathroom wrapped in a white terrycloth bathrobe. "I practically had to run around to get wet."

A knock on their door interrupted her.

"Girls! Curfew check!" their chaperon, Mrs. Blythe, called through the door.

Scarlett opened the door and smiled at the older woman. "You caught me just as I was about to say my prayers," she said.

"Oh, that's lovely." Mrs. Blythe clasped her hands with pleasure. "So few young people bother saying their prayers before bed anymore."

"It's such a shame, isn't it?" Dawn asked.

Mrs. Blythe looked surprised. "Well, yes, it is. Do you say prayers before bed, too, Dawn?"

"I surely do." Dawn nodded gravely. "After all, I have so much to be thankful for."

Mrs. Blythe's hands flew to her heart. "Isn't that lovely?"

"Dawn's attitude is an inspiration to us all," Scarlett-Caress intoned.

"I couldn't agree with you more," their chaperon said, "Night, night, girls. Sweet dreams." She shut the door behind her.

Scarlett-Caress gave Dawn an appraising look. "You're getting awfully good at this, aren't you?"

"I was taught by the master," Dawn said, as she wheeled herself into the bathroom to brush her teeth.

Scarlett-Caress dropped her towel, pulled on a white T-shirt, and climbed into bed. "I really do pray, you know," she said, yawning. "I pray to win every single pageant I'm in."

"You can't petition God with prayer," Dawn called from the bathroom.

"You can, too." Scarlett-Caress snuggled down under the

blankets. "I mean, otherwise, what's the point? Hurry up in there so we can turn out the lights."

Dawn wheeled herself back into the room. "I know for a fact that you can't petition God with prayer."

Scarlett-Caress groaned. "Okay, party pooper, how do you know you can't?"

"Because I have prayed to God every single day since my accident to let me walk again," Dawn told her. "And I'm still stuck in this chair."

Allison waited until she heard the heavy, regular rhythm of her roommate Donna Juarez's breathing, and knew the girl was finally asleep. That's when she crept out of bed and tiptoed to the bathroom. She shut the door quietly and switched on the bathroom light only long enough to dial a long-distance number on the phone. Then she turned the light off again and waited as the phone rang.

"Joe Lamont," a male voice barked into the phone.

"It's Allison Gaylord." She kept her voice low, careful not to wake her roommate. "What have you got for me?"

"Don't you believe in calling during business hours, Ms. Gaylord?" the man asked.

"Your business card says 'discreet handling of all your investigative needs twenty-four hours a day,'" Allison quoted, soundlessly pacing the bathroom floor in her bare feet. "I'm paying you a bundle, I might add, and I'm not paying for lip. Now, have you got something for me or am I firing you?"

"No need to get all huffy, Ms. Gaylord. I've got something."

Allison's hand tightened around the phone. "Good. What is it?"

"The party in question had a serious traffic violation last year in Shreveport, but her parents got it bumped down to a misdemeanor. She went to traffic school and did a community-service thing."

"I can't do anything with a traffic violation, you idiot!" Allison hissed.

And then Joe Lamont told Allison the precise nature of the traffic violation.

A malicious smile spread across her face. "Are you sure?"

"Positive."

"Can you get me proof?"

"Yeah, but it'll cost ya."

"I don't care," Allison said. "I'll pay whatever it costs. I need it by the end of this week."

"That's gonna be tough—"

"Just do it!" she ordered. "I'll call you late tomorrow night. And by that time I expect you to be able to tell me exactly when the proof will be in my hands. Is that clear?"

"Crystal," Mr. Lamont said. "But just one last thing."

"What?" Allison asked impatiently.

"You ever talk to me again like you talked to me tonight, I hang up and the whole thing is over. Ain't no amount of money worth your mouth, little girl. *Ciao*."

The detective hung up in Allison's ear.

She was too excited about the information she'd just received to dwell on it, though.

"I just hit the jackpot," she whispered aloud. "No one can stop me now. No one."

CHAPTER

12

It was twelve-thirty at night. Katie stood in front of room 2032 on the twentieth floor of the hotel, where Dean had told her to meet him. Her heart was hammering in her chest. She knocked softly.

Dean opened the door and she limped inside on her crutches as quickly as she could. He locked the door behind her. The room was tiny but well decorated, as if someone lived there full-time.

"Whose room is this?" she whispered, still terribly nervous.

"You don't need to whisper," Dean assured her. "My bud Kevin Daily lives here. He's house manager of the nightclub downstairs. I asked him to switch rooms with me for the night so we'd be as far away from everyone in the pageant as possible."

"That was nice of him," Katie said tensely.

"You can relax, Katie. Nothing bad is going to happen."

Katie smiled, but she was still filled with anxiety about all the rules she was breaking. With Willow's help, she had snuck out of her room after bed check, she was alone with

Dean, and on top of that, she was alone with Dean in a *hotel room*. With a *bed*. In the middle of the night. And just the other night she'd had a dream about him in which they were kissing, and he unbuttoned her shirt, and then they—

Okay, I don't sit on the bed, she decided, blushing at the memories of her own steamy dream. *I won't even* think *about the bed.*

"Sit," Dean told her. He sat on the bed and patted the spot next to him. "You need to rest your ankle."

"Oh, no, I can stand," Katie assured him quickly. "Let's just get started with the magic."

Dean stood and removed a top hat out of a sports sack that was lying on the floor. In the hat was a scruffy-looking, stuffed bunny.

"A personal friend of yours?" Katie asked, trying to make a joke.

"As a matter of fact, yes," Dean said. He held the blue bunny up to Katie. "Katie, this is Honey Bunny. Honey Bunny, my friend, Katie."

"And you just happen to have Honey Bunny with you here at the hotel?" Katie sounded dubious.

"This is the same rabbit I used in my magic act all through high school," Dean explained. "I wasn't about to carry around a live one. I guess you could call her my lucky rabbit. I carry my magic stuff with me everywhere. You never know when you might need to pick up a few bucks."

He picked up the top hat. "The first trick I'm going to teach you is how to pull a rabbit out of a hat."

"Okay, I'm watching."

"Magic works by fooling the eye of the audience," Dean explained as he stuffed Honey Bunny inside the top hat. "While the audience is distracted I manipulate the hat."

Quickly he waved his free hand—the left one—in front

of Katie's face. "Then I show the audience that there is absolutely nothing in the hat."

Dean turned the hat over and shook it, then he had Katie feel around the inside of the hat.

"There's nothing in there," she stated.

Dean waved the hat quickly around in the air. "Nothing in the hat, folks, the lady says there is nothing in the hat.

"Now we say the magic words, which are 'Katie makes it to the nationals', and . . . *voilà!* Reach into the hat, please."

Katie reached into the hat and pulled out the rabbit. "But how did you do that? That hat was empty!"

"The hand is quicker than the eye, I always say," Dean said. "Look." He showed Katie the false bottom of the top hat, under the silk.

"But I felt the bottom of the hat," she insisted.

"Of course you did," he agreed. "But when I waved the hat in the air, I compressed the silk and the cardboard underneath with just a flick of my finger. But you never saw it."

"And you think I can learn to do that?" Katie asked skeptically.

"Absolutely. Let me take you through it slowly, okay?"

First Dean broke the trick down into a sequence. Then, for the next hour, Katie attempted over and over to do the trick smoothly. And failed totally. Every time she tried, it was utterly obvious that she was manipulating the hat before she pulled the rabbit out. On her last effort, Honey Bunny actually fell completely out of the hat before she finished the trick.

"It's no use!" Katie cried. "I'm hopeless!" She sat on the bed and put her head in her hands. Her ankle hurt, she was exhausted and stressed out from all the events of the day, and she no longer cared about keeping her don't-even-sit-on-the-bed rule. Romance was the last thing on her mind, anyway.

Dean sat down next to her. "You've had a helluva day, huh?"

Katie nodded. "This was a crazy idea. I can't stay up all night and learn to do magic well enough to perform in front of all those judges tomorrow night."

Dean softly lifted a strand of her hair, then let it fall again. "Come on," he coaxed. "You don't really want to give up, do you?"

"No." She lifted her head to look at him. "But I don't want to look like an idiot, either."

"You could never look like an idiot," Dean told her.

Katie tried to smile. "I guess I should just be grateful I got this far and call it a day. I already won two thousand dollars. And that's about two thousand dollars more than I ever thought I'd win."

Dean was silent for a moment. "Maybe we could try a different trick," he then suggested.

Katie shook her head no. "It's two o'clock in the morning. Polimar Records is hosting a breakfast for us at the Opryland Hotel in exactly six hours."

She looked down at her hands. "It's just that I had this dream—I know it's silly—that I really could be one of the winners. I used to say it was just for the money. I really, really do need the money. But the truth is, I wanted to prove to myself that a girl like me could be a beauty queen, that winning Miss Virginia wasn't just some kind of crazy fluke. . . ."

"Why would you think that?"

She looked Dean clearly in the eye. "Because my family is poor, Dean. I mean really poor. The kind of people that other people call 'trailer trash.' Girls from my neighborhood become mothers at fourteen, or they get married and live in a junky trailer just like the junky trailer they grew up in, or, if they're really desperate, they become hookers. I knew one girl who married a rich man and moved away. But whenever she comes home to visit, her face is covered with bruises."

"None of those things will happen to you," Dean insisted.

"You're right," Katie agreed. "They won't. I'm going to find a way to go to college somehow. But the money from this pageant sure would have helped. And the girl who wins the nationals gets a four-year college scholarship. That's like some kind of perfect dream to me. . . ."

Dean reached out and cupped her face with his hand. "Do you have any idea how beautiful you are?"

"You don't have to say that—"

"I want to. From the very first moment I saw you, I knew you were special. It shines from your eyes, Katie. . . ."

He was so close to her now. His lips were so inviting. It would be so easy to just give in to all her feelings, to let herself feel the comfort of his strong arms. She longed for him to kiss her now. What difference did it make anymore?

Slowly, Dean brought his lips to hers. "Katie," he whispered hoarsely.

Yes, yes, kiss me, she thought. *Kiss me until I can't think anymore. Kiss me until—*

There was a knock on the door.

Katie let out a little shriek of fear and pulled away. Dean put his finger to his lips, indicating that she should be silent.

"Who is it?" he called out.

"It's Willow," came a hushed voice through the door.

Katie sat backward on the bed with relief as Dean went to open the door.

"Sorry—I know I probably scared the two of you to death," Willow said, hurrying into the room.

Katie sat up. "Did someone find out I was missing?"

"No, no, nothing like that," Willow assured her. She sat

on the chair at the small desk. "The two of you might think I'm crazy, but . . ."

"But what?" Dean asked, sitting back down next to Katie.

"Remember how you told me that Dean told you he could teach anyone to do great card tricks in a half hour?"

Katie nodded. "And I said card tricks couldn't work because playing cards are too small. No one in the audience, including the judges, would see the tricks."

"Right." Willow nodded. "Well, after you left, I started thinking about the pressure you're under. I know I couldn't learn to perform magic tricks in one night!"

"Neither can I," Katie admitted. "In fact, short of a miracle, I don't see how I can—"

"Maybe I found your miracle," Willow said.

Katie and Dean just stared at her.

"What I'm saying is," Willow continued, "what if the playing cards weren't too small?"

"But they are," Katie said slowly.

Willow smiled. "I remembered seeing this special on public television about magicians, and how they all got their supplies at this place in Los Angeles called the Magic Box. And I recalled how they said that the Magic Box is open twenty-four hours, and how one magician based his act on doing card tricks with these giant-sized playing cards he got at the Magic Box. . . ."

"You mean you called this magic store?" Katie asked.

Willow nodded. "Not only did I call, I ordered the super-king-size cards for you. Each card stands four feet high."

Katie couldn't believe what she had just heard. "You actually ordered—"

"Wait, hold on," Dean said. "It's a great idea, I admit, but the cards will never get here in time for the talent competition tomorrow night."

"Normally, that would be true," Willow agreed. "So I hired a private courier service, who guaranteed me that the cards will be here by two o'clock tomorrow afternoon."

"Willow, that must have cost a fortune," Katie protested. "I can't afford to pay for it."

"Please don't worry about it," Willow said. "My parents told me to use their credit card for anything that was really important. Well, this is really important."

"What will they say when they find you spent all this money for your roommate?" Katie asked.

"They'll say it's great," Willow replied, laughing. "I told you, they're the last of the great liberals. They consider it their patriotic duty to help others out financially."

"If it turns out you're wrong, I'll find some way to pay you back every penny," Katie promised.

"Deal," Willow said. "But you don't have to worry. I know my parents."

"You really did that for me?"

Willow nodded. "I know I should have asked you first, but . . . well . . . it would have been awkward, considering."

"I don't know what to say." Katie bit her lip to keep from crying. "It's about the nicest thing anyone every did for me, Willow."

"Hey, what's a best friend for?" Willow asked, her eyes shining.

Dean looked at Katie. "Card tricks with giant playing cards? I'd have to teach you on a regular-sized deck. And if we can't sneak away after the cards get here tomorrow afternoon, you'll have to wing it on stage."

"Can you really teach me some great card tricks in a half hour?" Katie asked him.

"You betcha," Dean said, grinning.

Katie looked at Willow. "Can you stay and help coach me

while I pretend I'm doing card tricks with invisible giant playing cards?"

"On crutches, with a limp?" Dean added.

"You betcha," Willow said, mimicking Dean.

"I must be the luckiest girl on the planet to have friends like you two." Tears were in Katie's eyes.

"You betcha!" Willow and Dean chorused at the same time.

Dean gave Katie a hug. "I'm the lucky one, Katie Laramie. Now let's get to work!"

CHAPTER

13

"I'd like to welcome our judges, the Miss Teen Spirit staff, and our honored guests to the preliminary talent portion of the Miss Teen Spirit Southern Regional Pageant," Mrs. Crownwell-Stevens said into the microphone in her low, musical voice. "The girl to be crowned the very first Miss Teen Spirit at the national pageant will be a very, very special girl, indeed. She will be intelligent, articulate, a leader in her community whose volunteer work inspires others, and she will be physically fit. In addition, she will be very talented. In fact, for those of you who do not know this, talent counts for twenty-five percent of each girl's final score.

"Tonight all thirty of the girls will be performing for you," Mrs. Crownwell-Stevens continued, "but in the pageant on Sunday, only the twelve girls with the top cumulative scores, our semifinalists, will perform. So, as you can see, a lot is at stake here tonight. There will be a short break after the first fifteen girls have performed, and coffee and refreshments will be served in the rear of the ballroom, followed by our second group of performances. The order in which the girls perform tonight was chosen randomly, by picking names out of a hat.

"I want to wish all our girls good luck, and I know you'll all be supportive as we present our preliminary talent competition. Thank you."

The audience of about a hundred people applauded enthusiastically. In addition to the judges seated in the front row, and the pageant staff, there was an invited audience, including the young country-music star Bryan White. Talent scouts and executives from every record label in Nashville were also present.

In the ballroom next door, all the girls were nervously watching Mrs. Crownwell-Stevens on a huge television monitor that had been set up. An assistant was to come and advise each girl when it was her turn to perform.

"I'm going to throw up." Donna Juarez groaned, holding her stomach.

"You'll be okay," Wanda Sue told her, patting her hand.

Donna pulled out her compact and looked at her face. "I knew it. I'm turning green I'm so sick."

"Well, that's okay," Wanda Sue replied. "You play the piano. The judges won't be able to see your face, anyway."

"Would you like me to ask for something to calm your stomach?" Michelle asked Donna.

"Nothing will help," Donna moaned. "And I'm on third!"

"Y'all, Becky Haas is on!" Shyanne called to them. Most of the girls gathered around the monitor to watch.

"Please welcome Miss Southern Brainiacs, Becky Haas, singing 'The Tennessee Waltz,'" Mrs. Crownwell-Stevens announced.

As the audience applauded, a young pageant assistant hurried into the room. "Michelle Evans?"

"I'm here," Michelle said, getting up.

"You're on second," the assistant told her. "Follow me."

Some girls called good luck to Michelle; others were glued to the monitor.

Becky stood center stage. She was wearing a floor-length kelly-green gown with long sleeves. Below her, in a makeshift orchestra pit, were grouped the musicians. Becky watched the conductor nervously, waiting for her musical cue.

"What a loser," Allison commented. "The fashion police should have her arrested."

"Shhh!" the other girls whispered.

They all listened carefully as Becky sang in a tremulous, operatic voice.

"Dang, she's good," Shyanne breathed.

No she isn't, Gigi thought critically. *Not that I'd ever say that out loud. But she's slightly off pitch and she's got a real problem with her vibrato. And on top of that, she doesn't know how to entertain the audience.*

Katie wasn't watching the television monitor. She was on the other side of the room, reviewing the card tricks with the giant cards in her mind.

"Are you okay?" Willow asked, coming over to her.

"No," Katie admitted. "I must have been crazy to think I could go out there and do this when I only got to practice once with the giant cards."

"It was nice of Mrs. Crownwell-Stevens to arrange the practice time for you, though," Willow said.

"You're not nervous at all, are you?" Katie accused her roommate.

"I am, too," Willow said. "I just don't let it show."

Katie took in her friend's beautiful, breathtakingly simple, Vera Wang gown. It was of the palest pink, fitted to the waist, and the full taffeta skirt flowed to the floor. Then she looked down at her own hot-pink leotard under a very short, flippy pink skater's skirt, covered with red hearts. It was the outfit she and Jane had picked out for her trampoline routine, but now Katie was sure it would look utterly ridiculous when she did her card tricks.

"I should never have worn this, Willow. I look like an idiot!"

"You look darling," Willow insisted.

Becky finished singing, and Michelle was introduced. She strode confidently out onto the stage, looking cute, tiny, muscular, and fit in her Stars and Stripes leotard.

The orchestra began to play her music, a medley of Gershwin tunes. Michelle's gymnastics were dazzling.

"Okay, so she's strong," Allison admitted. "She's not exactly graceful. She needs breast implants or no one will ever be able to tell she's a girl."

"Would you kindly shut up?" Jennifer Worden suggested bluntly.

After two more girls had performed, the assistant reentered the room and called Scarlett-Caress's name.

"Here I go," she said to Dawn, kissing her roommate on the cheek. "Wish me luck!"

"You don't need luck," Dawn told her. "You'll be great."

"Plus I've got my handy pitch pipe!" Scarlett-Caress said, holding it up. It was a trick she had learned from a pageant-head at her very first pageant. Sometimes, if she started to feel nervous right before she sang, it was hard for her to pick out her starting pitch from the orchestra. So right before she went on stage, she played her pitch on a pitch pipe.

"Please welcome Miss Teen Spirit Pride of the South, Scarlett-Caress Latham, singing 'All That Jazz' from the Broadway musical *Chicago*," Mrs. Crownwell-Stevens announced.

As the audience applauded, Scarlett-Caress lifted the pitch pipe to her mouth and blew into it.

A tiny, dull, off-pitch sound came out.

She tried again. Another small, low sound.

The applause was dying down now, and Scarlett-Caress had to rush out onto the stage. She felt flustered at the failure of her pitch pipe. The orchestra struck up her introduction. She couldn't hear her starting note.

When her cue came, Scarlett-Caress spoke the words to the first line, a smile plastered on her face.

No, no this can't be happening! she thought as she desperately tried to find the right pitch.

She spoke the second line.

And then she heard it! Yes! The pianist was hitting the melody line hard, trying to help her out.

She came in smoothly on the third line, singing perfectly on pitch.

And then she sailed through the rest of the flirty song, and finished big, one shapely leg peeking out of the slit in her sexy black skirt.

The audience applauded, Scarlett-Caress grinned and bowed, managing to look both confident and tremendously humble at the same time. Then she ran off stage.

The first thing she did was to find the pitch pipe she had dropped right before she went on. She knocked it hard against her hand.

Water flew out. Water that didn't belong in a pitch pipe. Water that would make the pitch pipe play a low, dull sound instead of a pitch.

It didn't take Scarlett-Caress long to solve this mystery.

The Virus had struck.

Dawn was slated to go on tenth. The other girls were gathered around the monitor, watching and listening. Her flute solo was lyrical and lovely.

Beth went on fourteenth. She played an extremely difficult solo for violin by Tchaikovsky, and she played it
flawlessly.

Gigi was waiting in the wings, her palms wet with
nervous perspiration. She had drawn the last spot in the first
group. She could tell that the audience was restless from
sitting for so long, that they needed a break, and this only
made her feel even more nervous.

When Mrs. Crownwell-Stevens finished introducing her,
Gigi held her head high and strode out onto the stage.

"Go, Gigi," Katie said, forgetting about her own nerves
long enough to watch the monitor and root for her friend.
"Doesn't she look great?" she asked Dawn excitedly,
grabbing her hand.

"No one sings in a sequined dress in the prelims," Allison
scoffed. "Talk about cheap!"

As the orchestra played the introduction to her gospel-
music number, Gigi closed her eyes for the briefest of
moments. She felt the spirit fill her.

And then she sang.

A hushed silence filled the room where the girls were
waiting. Even Allison was rendered speechless.

Because Gigi was spectacular. And they all knew it.

When the last soaring note of her performance finished
ringing in the air, for a moment the audience couldn't even
applaud. They were too overwhelmed.

But when they did applaud, it was a wall of sound. People
yelled "Bravo!" others whistled or stomped their feet. Gigi
took two bows, then ran offstage with the audience still
clapping for her.

"She was fantastic!" Beth screamed from the waiting
room, jumping up and down and applauding as if Gigi could
hear her. "Wasn't she fantastic?"

"Beth, this is the most excited I've ever seen you get about anything," Dawn teased her.

The audience wouldn't stop applauding, and Gigi ran out onstage for one more bow.

"You go, girl!" Beth yelled at the monitor, then she whistled through her teeth.

"I think rooming with Gigi has had an effect on her." Dawn giggled to Katie.

When Gigi returned to their room, flushed with success, everyone gathered around to tell her how wonderful she had been. Everyone except Allison.

The Virus stood alone in the corner and eyed Gigi across the room, berating herself.

I might have made a fatal error, she was thinking. *I figured she was way too flashy to be a contender. But now I see she's really in the running.*

I may have to do something about that.

"Allison Gaylord?" the assistant called. "You're first after the dessert break."

"Thank you so much!" Allison called back.

She got her baton and walked backstage to wait.

Before she knew it, the break was over, and the audience had settled back into their seats. As Mrs. Crownwell-Stevens introduced her she plastered a huge smile on her face, then she ran out on stage with all the energy in the world.

Her routine went flawlessly. She caught every baton throw. When she lit the ends of both batons with fire, the audience murmured appreciatively.

"Too bad she didn't catch her hair on fire," Scarlett-Caress commented, watching the monitor. She was sure Allison had gotten ahold of her pitch pipe and put water in it.

Of course, I can't prove it, she thought. *Which is exactly the way The Virus operates.*

Allison moved into her spectacular finish. She threw the fiery batons high into the air, did a flip that ended in a split, and caught both batons. The audience applauded enthusiastically, and Allison waved at them and then applauded them before she ran offstage.

Following Allison was Wanda Sue Burnett, belly-dancing in diaphanous sheer purple pants that barely covered her hips, and a purple bra top. All the girls agreed they had never seen anything quite like it. Then Shyanne Derringer came out in a cowgirl outfit entirely covered in rhinestones, and did rope tricks while the orchestra played the theme from the old television show *Bonanza.*

Waiting in the wings was Katie. She had sweated so much from fear that she was now freezing cold. Offstage a stagehand was holding her giant deck of cards, waiting for Shyanne to finish so he could set them up.

"I can't remember any of the card tricks!" Katie realized, yelping out loud. "My mind is totally blank!"

She closed her eyes and tried to picture the cards and what she was supposed to do with them. She had gone over and over it with Dean and Willow.

First you turn over six cards, she reminded herself. *No, first you ask someone from the* audience *to pick six cards—*

"Hey, that's you!"

Katie opened her eyes.

"You're on, kid," the stagehand said as he hurried onto the stage to set up Katie's cards.

Katie took a deep breath, put her crutches more firmly under her armpits, and limped out onto the stage.

"Good evening," she said into the microphone, smiling into the blinding lights. "You might be wondering about the crutches. Well, I'd like to tell you that I did something exciting, like falling off the back of Bryan White's motor-cycle—"

The audience chuckled appreciatively.

"—but the truth is that when we all got to meet Bryan a few days ago at a luncheon, I was so starstruck I couldn't even ask for his autograph, much less ask for a ride on his motorcycle. What happened is, I sprained my ankle practicing my trampoline routine."

"Awwww," the audience groaned sympathetically.

"So I'll be sharing something else with you tonight." She looked behind her at the four-foot-high boards. "Believe it or not, those are playing cards. And I'm about to show you three of the world's greatest card tricks. Can I get a volunteer from the audience to help me out?"

To Katie's shock, Bryan White bounded up onto the stage. Her jaw fell open.

"But . . . but . . ." she stammered.

"I'm sorry you didn't get a ride on my motorcycle," Bryan said into the microphone. "But the truth is, I don't own a motorcycle."

The audience laughed.

"I made that up," Katie confessed. "But the part about being scared to get your autograph was true."

Bryan smiled. "I'll tell you what, after the card tricks, you can give me *your* autograph!"

The audience chuckled again, and Katie could feel that they were on her side. She went through the card tricks, limping on her crutches from card to card. Bryan kept offering to turn the cards for her so she wouldn't have to limp around, but she refused his help, and without them really trying, it somehow turned into a kind of slapstick-comedy routine.

When she finished her tricks, Bryan kissed her on the

cheek and the audience applauded warmly before she
hobbled off the stage.

Well, at least I got through it, she told herself. When she
hobbled into the waiting room next door she was practically
limp with relief.

"Girlfriend, that was too funny," Gigi told her, hugging
her hard.

"Did you even know Bryan White was in the audience?"
Dawn asked her.

"You know, I can't even remember!" Katie fell into the
nearest chair. "I am just so glad it's over."

"I hope you don't think the audience was laughing *with*
you," Allison said, sidling over to Katie. "Because they
were laughing *at* you."

"Allison, you had better get out of my face," Katie told
her. Allison gave her a haughty look and walked away.

"Katie, you were wonderful." Willow leaned over to hug
her roommate.

Did Katie smell alcohol on her roommate's breath, or was
she imagining it?

"Well, it's not like what I did compares to a real talent,"
she said, pulling out of Willow's embrace. "But I did the
best I could." Her eyes searched Willow's. "Are you okay?"

"I'm fine," Willow replied, a puzzled look on her face. "I
mean, I'm nervous, but I'm fine."

Have you been drinking again? Katie wanted to ask.
*Please tell me the truth. You've helped me so much. Maybe
I can help you.*

She longed to say it. But she couldn't. What if it made
Willow angry? Or offended? Or what if Katie was wrong?

"Willow Rose Harrison?" the assistant called. "You're
next."

"Good luck, Willow," Katie told her.

"Thanks."

Willow hurried toward the rear entrance to the stage. *Thank God I managed to hide that bottle in the ladies' room,* she told herself. *I feel so much better now.*

After her introduction, Willow floated onto the stage. The orchestra played the introduction to her song, "Somewhere Over the Rainbow."

Her clear, soprano voice filled the room with its sweetness. Standing there in her exquisite pale pink dress, her white-gold hair streaming down her shoulders, she looked perfect. She sounded perfect.

She is *perfect,* Katie thought, watching her on the monitor.

"Well, after Willow wins, that leaves five open spots for the nationals," Donna Juarez observed from behind Katie.

"Dang, Willow could win the whole shooting match," Shyanne admitted.

No one had to second the motion. Everyone knew it was true. Willow Rose Harrison really *could* be crowned Miss Teen Spirit.

I must be crazy, thinking that Willow is an alcoholic, Katie decided, watching her roommate's ethereal face on the monitor as she sang the final, stirring notes of the famous song. *It's just not possible. She's too wonderful. Nothing can keep her from succeeding.*

Allison, of course, was watching the monitor, too. And what she was thinking was that it was even worse than she had feared. Willow was great. Beyond great.

She really could win it all, Allison realized, her eyes narrowing. *I've got to stop Willow here, before she gets to the nationals.*

Because I'm going to be the first Miss Teen Spirit. And nothing and no one is going to stand in my way.

"*T*his is how I've got it charted right now." Beth scrambled up from the floor to the bed so that the others could see what she'd written. "The judges have done our prelim scores on talent and platform speeches. They've given us private interview scores, too, of course, but I can't access those scores since they are, by definition, done in private."

"Forget trying to win Miss Teen Spirit, Beth," Dawn told her. "You should run for President of the United States."

"The thought *has* crossed my mind," Beth admitted.

It was Friday night, and once again the gang had come together in Dawn and Scarlett-Caress's room for a gabfest.

Everyone was gathered around Beth's chart except Gigi, who was lost in thought.

Only an hour until curfew. After that, I sneak out to be with Trey. Soon I'll be in his arms, his lips will be on mine. . . .

"Gigi, are you on this planet?" Dawn asked, nudging the other girl in the ribs.

"Oh, sure," Gigi said. "What does the chart say?"

"Beth has you ranked number one for talent," Dawn said.

"For real?" Gigi asked happily.

"Well, it was a toss-up between you and Wanda Sue," Beth teased.

"See now, your sense of humor has truly improved since I came into your life, Beth," Gigi said.

"You've got Willow down for second," Shyanne said, peering over Katie's shoulder.

"Right," Beth said. "Third place is a toss-up. Actually, for pure musicianship, I'm probably first. But since I have no reason to think the judges know a lot about classical violin, I put myself as tied for third."

"With Dawn and me!" Shyanne noted.

"Hey, what am I, sweetcakes, chopped liver?" Scarlett-Caress was pouting.

"You spoke the first two lines of your song," Beth reminded her.

Scarlett-Caress was too proud to tell them her suspicions about the pitch pipe. The only one she had confided in was Dawn, and she knew Dawn would never tell.

"I'll have you know that was on purpose," Scarlett-Caress told them huffily. "Besides, Beth, no offense, but your little ol' chart is utterly worthless. You are looking at talent from an intellectual point of view. But that's not how the judges look at it."

"How do *they* look at it?" Katie asked.

"I can tell you what the pageant bible says," Shyanne said eagerly. " 'Talent is to be judged on creativity, uniqueness, stage presence, personality, and training,' " she quoted.

"Personality would be Katie," Dawn said. "How did you ever come up with the idea of giant-card tricks?"

"Yeah, and how did you get it all together so fast?" Gigi wanted to know. "When we left your room you were ready to give up."

"Two angels came to my rescue," Katie said, smiling at Willow.

"Willow and . . ." Gigi mused. And then it dawned on her. "Dean! It was Dean!"

"I'm not saying." Katie pursed her lips.

"Ooo, I know it was Dean," Gigi teased, jumping around the room. "This is just too romantic!"

"I haven't even kissed him, Geeg," Katie protested, blushing.

"Yet," Gigi added, wiggling her eyebrows at Katie.

"Y'all just remember," Scarlett-Caress said, "charisma counts. It's gotten me where I am today, thank you very much. That means all of us are contenders."

"How did you rate the platform speeches?" Katie asked Beth.

"Am I talking to myself?" Scarlett-Caress asked. "All of that doesn't matter. The judges get a feeling about a girl. They like her. They root for her. They can see her in the crown. And it doesn't matter if three girls are more talented and four girls give better speeches."

"So then, what you're saying is that the judging is arbitrary, capricious, and utterly unfair," Beth concluded.

Scarlett-Caress smiled. "If I'm one of the six that goes to nationals, I'm sure the judging is just perfect."

Gigi got up and yawned dramatically. "I'm beat. I think I'll go crash." She gave Beth a significant look.

"Me, too," Beth said, slipping her chart into the pocket of her jeans.

The group broke up, and Gigi and Beth hurried back to their room.

"Gigi, are you sure you want to risk this?" Beth asked as Gigi ran around getting ready for her date with Trey.

"I love him, Beth," Gigi replied, spraying herself with her favorite perfume.

"But if you get caught—"

"You know, you are getting boring with this," Gigi said. "Has anyone ever come to our room after bed check since we got here?"

"No," Beth admitted.

"So then, take a chill pill." She held a cropped red suede shirt up to her chest. "Is this good?"

"It's alluring," Beth decided.

"Alluring is good." Gigi laughed, then pulled off her T-shirt and pulled on the red top. She had hardly finished dressing for her secret date when Mrs. Drummond's knock sounded on the door.

Gigi took a flying leap into her bed and pulled the covers up to her chin. Then Beth opened the door.

"Bed check, girls," the older woman announced, peering into their room.

"I was just about to brush my teeth and crawl into bed," Beth assured her.

Mrs. Drummond peered at Gigi. "Young lady, do you have makeup on?"

"I . . . uh . . ." Gigi stammered.

"I keep telling her how bad it is for her skin to go to bed with her cosmetics on, Mrs. Drummond," Beth ad-libbed. "Believe me, I plan to make sure she washes thoroughly before I turn this light out."

Mrs. Drummond smiled. "That's what we like to see— you girls looking out for each other. Sleep tight, girls." She shut the door behind her.

"Good save." Gigi sighed with relief as she got out of bed and slipped her shoes on.

Beth sat on her bed. "I don't have a good feeling about this, Gigi."

"Well, I have enough good feelings about it for both of

us." Gigi looked at her watch. "How long do you think I need to wait to make sure the old biddy is asleep?"

"Thirty minutes, to be safe."

"That's forever," Gigi said, bouncing impatiently on her bed.

After exactly thirty minutes had passed, she finally peered out into the hallway. It was empty. Beth gave her a hug and warned her again to be careful, and then Gigi flew down the hall to the elevators. She could already picture herself in Trey's arms.

Willow stood in the bathroom and reread the note addressed to her that had been slipped under her door.

MEET ME IN THE TENTH-FLOOR STAIRWELL TONIGHT FIFTEEN MINUTES AFTER BED CHECK IF YOU KNOW WHAT'S GOOD FOR YOU.

The note wasn't signed.

It has to be from Allison, Willow thought. *Somehow she found my stash of liquor. That has to be it.*

"You ready to turn out the light, Willow?" Katie called.

"Sure," Willow called back, still staring at the note. She folded it and put it in the pocket of her robe, then stepped into the bedroom.

"I am so exhausted," Katie said, yawning, snuggling her head against her pillow. "You must be, too."

"I am," Willow agreed tonelessly. She sat on the edge of her bed.

Katie could tell something was on her roommate's mind. "What's up?"

"Oh, nothing."

"Then why are you sitting on your bed instead of in your bed?" Katie asked.

Willow got up. "I need to go out for a few minutes."

Katie sat up. "Are you crazy? We've already had bed check."

"I won't be long," Willow assured her, heading for the door.

"But—"

"Really, I'm fine. I'll be back before you even know I'm gone."

Willow hurried down the hall, past the elevators, and opened the door to the stairwell.

No one was there.

"Well, if it isn't Miss Perfect," came a voice from above her.

Willow looked up. Slowly descending the stairs was none other than Allison Gaylord.

The Virus.

"I have no idea what this is about, and you have exactly two minutes to talk to me," Willow told her.

Allison smiled maliciously in her face. "You are in no position to call the shots here," she jeered. "If you didn't think you were in a heap of trouble, you never would have broken curfew to come meet me."

"You broke curfew, too," Allison pointed out.

"If anyone asks, I simply ran down the hall to check on my dear friend Wanda Sue," Allison said, leaning against the wall. "She'll corroborate that, by the way. The poor thing has terrible cramps."

"What is it that you want?" Willow snapped.

"Not much," Allison drawled lazily. "I just want you to drop out of the pageant."

"You want *what*?"

"Tomorrow would be a good time to drop out," Allison mused. "Or Sunday morning . . . I'm all right with that, too."

"You're out of your mind." Willow turned and reached for the door.

"Before you go, I'd really like to know your opinion on drunk drivers," Allison said.

Willow's hand was still on the door, her back to Allison. "What are you talking about?"

"You know. People who get drunk and then deliberately get behind the wheel of a car. I think it's just plain criminal, don't you? I think a person who does something like that should be exposed for the true lowlife that she is."

Willow's hand began to shake. "I don't know what you're talking about."

"No? Well then, let me refresh your memory." Allison's eyes shone wickedly in the light of the stairwell. "Last year a certain Miss Willow Rose Harrison, daughter of two very famous hotshots in the Democratic Party of Louisiana, was arrested on a DWI —that's Driving While Intoxicated, in case you aren't familiar with the lingo. Shall I continue?"

"Go on." Willow tried to keep her voice even.

"Well, the shock of it all grows, boys and girls," Allison said. "Because not only was Willow Rose drunk as a skunk, she ran into a little boy who had dashed out into the street to get his ball."

"He came from between two parked cars," Willow said. "I couldn't see him—"

"The little boy's arm was broken," Allison continued.

"But that's all," Willow said quickly, her voice high and strained. "He wasn't badly hurt. We paid all his medical bills."

"Aren't you wonderful to have done that?" Allison asked sarcastically. "But let me continue the story. Famous mummy and daddy weren't about to let their baby's records be stained forever by this nasty little episode, so they used their political influence to get the charges against their darling daughter reduced to reckless driving. Darling daughter went to traffic school and did some community service, and— here's the best part—her parents even managed to get the whole nasty little episode erased from her records. Poof! Perfect Willow is perfect again."

Willow finally turned around to face her enemy. "I went into rehab after that, Allison."

"Isn't that nice. And soon you're going to drop out of the pageant, or else Mrs. Crownwell-Stevens will be getting quite an earful about you."

Willow stood tall. "You don't have any proof."

"Oh, don't I?" Allison taunted her. "I have a copy of the original arrest report, and you know I'll use it. So just say bye-bye Miss Teen Spirit, Willow, and go back home where Mummy and Daddy can take care of you."

Willow stared into Allison's eyes. The only emotion she saw reflected in them was hate. "Do you really want to win that badly?"

"Of course," Allison said. "And so do you."

"I feel sorry for you, Allison. I really do." Willow turned and opened the door, and she was gone.

Allison stood by herself a moment, thinking.

Willow didn't say whether or not she'd drop out, she realized. *But there's no way she'll risk it. I hope. Because I was bluffing about having backup. That stupid private detective couldn't get me any records of the arrest.*

The truth is, I don't really have any proof at all.

"Oh, Trey," Gigi murmured, locked in his embrace. "I can't believe you're really here!"

"I am," he assured her, nuzzling her neck. "God, I missed you so much, baby."

Wide-eyed, Gigi looked around the penthouse suite at the Rowen Towers Grand Plaza Hotel. "This must have cost you a fortune!"

"Since we only had one night together, I wanted to make it special," Trey said.

Gigi ran to the window and looked out at the sparkling lights of the Nashville skyline. Then she turned back to take in the gigantic suite. The two large rooms were carpeted in lush forest green, with rich tapestry green-and-burgundy shades to block out the world. The light from a crystal chandelier above them had been dimmed, casting a sexy, golden glow over the room.

And in the next room was a huge, tapestry-covered bed.

Trey reached for her hand. "Come on in here, Geeg."

He led her into the bedroom.

Next to the bed was an ice bucket. A sweating bottle was nestled in the ice.

Am I really going through with this? Gigi asked herself nervously. *I mean, am I really ready to go* all *the way through with this?*

"Great room," she said, "but you know I don't drink."

"It's sparkling apple cider." Trey lifted the bottle from the ice bucket. "No alcohol." He popped it open and poured some into two crystal champagne flutes. Then he clinked his glass against hers.

"To us," he said softly.

"To us." Gigi took a sip of the sparkling cider. The bubbles tickled her nose.

Trey went to the CD player that was recessed into the entertainment center, pushed a button, and the sounds of mellow jazz filled the room. Then he lit a fat green candle that was on the nightstand, and turned out the light.

"This is like something out of a movie." Gigi giggled nervously.

"I want to make it perfect for you," Trey said. He took her glass of cider and placed it on the nightstand beside his. Then he took her hand and slowly lowered her to the bed.

"Just hold me a minute, Trey," Gigi whispered as she nuzzled against the guy she loved.

"I love holding you," he murmured.

For a long time they lay there together. She felt so safe, so protected, lying in his strong arms.

"We've got to stop hiding from your parents, Gigi," Trey whispered into her hair. "I want to stand up to them like a man, and tell them how much I love you."

Gigi pulled away enough so that she could see into his eyes. "Do you? Love me?"

"How can you even ask me that? Gigi, someday I'm going to marry you."

Marry? Gigi thought. He wants to marry me? Then he must really, truly love me! But I'm not ready to get married!

"Marriage isn't exactly in my plans for a long, long time," she told him.

"Mine neither," Trey agreed. "So let's just practice the good parts of it until then."

Slowly he lowered his mouth to hers. He kissed her gently, then more passionately, until she was lost in the ecstasy of his embrace.

Then he began trailing kisses along her stomach as he lifted, inch by inch, her red suede shirt.

"I . . . I . . ." Gigi stammered.

"Shhh," Trey whispered. Her shirt was up above her bra now. "It's okay." He lifted the shirt over her head.

She let him. It all felt so unreal, as if it were happening to someone else.

"Gigi, you are so beautiful," Trey said huskily as he stared down at her in the candlelight.

He undid the snap on her jeans. His large, smooth hand

rested on the flat of her stomach as he kissed her neck softly.

"Trey, I . . ."

"What?" He was kissing her shoulder now.

"I . . . I don't think I'm ready to . . ."

"Shhhh," he murmured. He pulled his T-shirt over his head. His gorgeous brown skin was pulled taut over his sinewy muscles.

He reached to unzip her jeans.

Gigi bolted upright.

"What?" Trey asked.

"Trey, I'm not . . . I can't . . ."

He dropped his hands. "You're not ready?"

"I'm . . . I thought I was, but . . . it's not that I don't love you . . ."

Trey sighed and wrapped his arms around her. "Gigi, it's okay."

"Are you sure?"

"Well, I'm not going to say that I'm not disappointed, but it's okay. We won't make love until you're ready."

"Why are you being so nice about this?" Gigi asked, holding him tight.

Trey chuckled softly. "I guess you already know the answer to that, girl. Or did you think I only love you for your hot body?"

"Oh, Trey," Gigi breathed, her heart melting. She gave him a sizzling kiss.

Just then the phone rang, startling them both.

For a second they just stared at each other.

"It has to be for you," Gigi finally said. "The only person who knows where I am is Beth. And she'd never call, unless . . ."

The phone kept ringing.

Finally, Trey answered it. "Hello?"

"Trey? It's Beth. I have to speak to Gigi."

Wordlessly, Trey handed the phone to Gigi. Her heart was pounding as she put it to her ear. "Beth? What happened?"

"Gigi, you've got to get back here right away."

"What happened?"

"Five minutes ago Mrs. Drummond pounded on our door. She did a second bed check! She said it was because you had makeup on when you were in bed and she wasn't born yesterday. I told her you had a terrible stomachache and you didn't want to wake her, so you went downstairs to see if that little shop in the lobby was open so you could get some Pepto-Bismol. She just went downstairs to look for you. Oh, Gigi, I don't think she bought a word of it!"

"How am I going to get into the hotel without her seeing me?" Gigi asked, panicked.

"Try the freight entrance," Beth said. "I have no idea if it's open or not. I don't even know where it is, but I'll find it. I'll meet you there and let you in if I can. And Gigi, hurry!"

Gigi hung up the phone and jumped off the bed. She threw her shirt on, snapped her jeans, and stepped into her shoes, babbling what had happened to Trey.

"I should come with you," he said, reaching for his sneakers. "I'm not letting you take this rap alone."

"No, stay here," Gigi told him. "Beth is going to try and sneak me in. Oh, God, I am so screwed."

She gave Trey a final kiss, promising to call him when she could to tell him what had happened. Then she sprinted down the hall, got on the elevator, and prayed.

Please don't let me have blown everything.

She was able to get a taxi quickly, and the streets of Nashville were empty as the cab sped back to her hotel. She made the driver stop down the block from the hotel, just in case Mrs. Drummond had people watching the front door. Then she threw a twenty-dollar bill at the man and ran around the block to try to locate a freight entrance to the hotel.

Yes! There in the alley, a door leading into the rear of the hotel. Gigi tried it. It was locked. She pounded on it, hoping Beth was standing on the other side, waiting to let her in.

There was no answer.

She pounded harder. "Beth! Please open the door! Beth!"

Silence.

Gigi leaned against the building, breathing hard. *I don't know what to do. I've got to figure out what to do!*

This time she kicked the door as hard as she could. Someone, *anyone,* had to open it for her!

And then, finally, someone did.

He was a cop, in a blue uniform.

And standing behind him, staring at Gigi, was Mrs. Drummond.

CHAPTER

15

It was Sunday morning. Gigi stood with her friends in the lobby of the hotel, her suitcases at her feet. A storm of activity was whirling around the forlorn little group. The pageant was set to begin in six hours, but some family and friends of contestants were already arriving, happily greeting each other with excited hugs and kisses. The bellhops were piling load after load of luggage onto their carts and escorting people up to their rooms.

In the center of this gale of excitement was Gigi. Katie, Dawn, Beth, Shyanne, and Scarlett-Caress surrounded her. Willow was suffering from a terrible headache, so she had said her good-byes to Gigi before she went downstairs.

Gigi had been kicked out of the pageant.

Mrs. Drummond had been savvy enough to have had both entrances to the hotel watched the night before so there had been no way that Gigi could sneak in. Beth had been unable to come to her aid. When she saw the pageant officials at the doors, she intelligently went back up to their room . . . but not before one of the officials had spotted her.

Early Saturday morning, Gigi had met with Mrs. Drummond and Mrs. Crownwell-Stevens. But really, what possible excuse could she offer? Finally, she had just told them the truth, and begged them not to take it out on Beth, who had tried to cover for her.

Mrs. Drummond was all for disqualifying both girls. But Mrs. Crownwell-Stevens decided that Beth could stay. Gigi's parents would have to come and retrieve her before the pageant began Sunday afternoon.

Calling her parents to say that she had been kicked out of the pageant for breaking the rules was the hardest thing Gigi had ever done. She cried through the entire conversation. She knew how much she had let them down.

And now, waiting for them to pick her up, she was still crying. Her friends couldn't think of anything to say to console her.

"I can't believe I was so stupid," Gigi said for the hundredth time, blowing her nose again. "This was such a big chance for me, and I blew it. After this, my father will probably lock me in the house every day after school. He'll never trust me again."

"Look who's coming this way," Dawn said under her breath.

Gigi turned. Mrs. Crownwell-Stevens was heading right toward them.

"What does she want to do, rub it in?" Gigi asked.

The older woman, already impeccably dressed for the pageant, approached Gigi.

"Gigi, I'm sorry this happened. I want you to know I think you're a very talented young lady."

"Thank you," Gigi managed.

"Evidently other people think so, too." She held out a white business card. "The president of Gemtone Music was in the audience during the talent preliminaries and he heard you sing. He asked me to give you his card."

Gigi took it. The raised, embossed letters read JIMMY STEVENS, PRESIDENT, GEMTONE MUSIC.

"Some of the biggest gospel acts in the world are their clients!" Gigi exclaimed.

"He wants you to call him, Gigi," Mrs. Crownwell-Stevens continued. "And I don't think he wants to talk to you about the Miss Teen Spirit Pageant."

"Gigi!" Shyanne cried. "He's gonna make you a star!"

All the girls started talking at once.

"I hope you'll stay in touch and let me know what happens," Mrs. Crownwell-Stevens told Gigi.

"I will," Gigi promised. "And . . . I want you to know I'm sorry I let everyone down."

"I'm sorry, too," the older woman said. "I think mostly you let yourself down. But often we end up learning more from our failures than we do from our successes, Gigi. And I have a feeling you have a wonderful future ahead of you . . . if you develop better judgment." She gave the girl a hug and walked away.

"She's really elegant," Shyanne decided.

"For an over-the-hill pageant-head, I say she's all right," Scarlett-Caress admitted.

"There's my parents' car." Gigi was peering out the front glass door of the hotel. "I asked them not to come in—not that they wanted to, anyway."

"Excuse me," Scarlett-Caress called to a bellhop. "Could you be a sweetheart and take this luggage out to that car for my friend?"

"Sure!" the young bellhop said, clearly dazzled by Scarlett-Caress.

Gigi turned to her friends. "Well, I guess this is it."

"I hate good-byes." Beth's tone was mournful.

Gigi hugged each of them in turn. "This isn't good-bye.

All of you are going to the nationals, I just know it. And I'll find some way to get there so I can root you on."

From behind her, Gigi felt a tap on her shoulder. She turned around. Standing there, looking so handsome that it took her breath away, was Trey.

"Trey! What are you doing here?" she cried.

"That seems pretty obvious to me," he answered, scratching his chin.

"But you were supposed to be on the tour bus, on your way to Georgia!"

"Well, I guess I can get there in time for tonight's gig," Trey said. "I had something important to do first. Like be with you when you face your parents."

Tears welled up in Gigi's eyes. "Oh, Trey," she said softly, and melted into his arms.

"I guess this is the African god she calls her boyfriend," Beth said.

Gigi laughed, and quickly introduced Trey to her friends.

"Nice to meet you," he told them, then turned back to Gigi. "You ready for us to face the music with your parents? Together?"

"I'm ready," Gigi said.

And with one last look at her friends, Gigi and Trey headed out the door.

Beth looked as if she was going to cry.

"No time for tears, sweetums," Scarlett-Caress scolded her. "Your eyes will be red and puffy for the pageant."

"It won't be half as much fun without Gigi." Beth groaned.

"I adore her, too," Scarlett-Caress said. "But let's face it, with her talent and bubbly personality, she was a shoo-in to be one of the six winners going on to nationals. Now all six spots are open. Girls, let's go get ready to knock 'em dead!"

Katie was already missing Gigi as she let herself into her room. She looked at her watch and felt butterflies rise up in her stomach. Jane would be arriving soon. The pageant was going to start in just a few hours; she simply had to put Gigi out of her mind.

Balancing herself on one foot, she pulled off her T-shirt and jeans, then hopped over to the bathroom door and tapped on it. "Willow? I need to get in and take a shower when you're done."

There was no answer.

A terrible dread filled Katie's heart.

She knocked again. "Willow?"

No answer.

Please don't let her be drunk, please don't let her be drunk, Katie chanted to herself, and slowly opened the bathroom door.

Her heart sank. Willow was drunk.

It was like a replay of the time they had met. Because once again Willow was a mess, lying on the bathroom floor. This time, though, she was naked, her white terrycloth robe flung over the edge of the sink. An empty bottle of vodka lay near her hand.

And this time, Willow was out cold.

Katie knelt down and shook her roommate. "Willow? . . . Willow?"

She got no response.

For one terrorized moment she was afraid the girl was dead. But then she felt for her pulse, and found it.

Keeping the panic down, Katie tried to drag Willow across the bathroom floor, to get her into the bathtub and give her a cold shower. But given her limited use of one foot, Willow seemed like a deadweight. Katie couldn't budge her.

For a moment she was so angry at Willow that she felt like just leaving her there in a heap.

How can a girl who has absolutely everything throw it all away like this? Katie wondered. *This is not my problem!*

Then she immediately felt guilty as she remembered all the wonderful things Willow had done for her. She couldn't possibly be that small-minded. And besides, Willow was her best friend.

Katie hopped over to the phone and called room service. She ordered two large pots of black coffee. Then she dialed Dawn and Scarlett-Caress's room.

"Hello?" Dawn answered the phone.

"It's Katie. Can you come down to my room right away?"

"I'm getting ready for the pageant," Dawn said. "You should be, too. Scarlett-Caress says that less than five hours of prep time is deadly."

"It's an emergency," Katie said. "It's Willow."

"I'll be right there."

Within five minutes Dawn was knocking at the door. "What's the crisis?" she asked, wheeling herself in.

"It's Willow," Katie said. "She's drunk. She's passed out in the bathroom. I ordered up some black coffee. But I need help to get her into the shower."

Dawn wheeled herself toward the bathroom, but because the room wasn't wheelchair accessible, the door opening to the bathroom wasn't large enough for her wheelchair.

"I should have thought of that," Katie muttered angrily, biting her lower lip. "I guess I should call Beth."

"Just because I can't use my legs doesn't mean I can't help you," Dawn told her. "Now, keep your weight on your good foot and put your hands under my armpits and lift me. I'm not that heavy."

Katie did what Dawn told her to do. Then, as Dawn directed her, she half dragged Dawn to the edge of the bathtub.

"Good," Dawn said. "Now get behind Willow and lift her legs. I can reach her arms from here."

"But how can you—?"

"Katie, I have tremendous upper-body strength. Believe me, I can lift her." Dawn reached down and grabbed Willow under her arms. Then, with Katie positioned at Willow's legs, they managed to get the unconscious girl into the tub. Clearly, Dawn was doing most of the lifting.

Just then there was a knock on the door.

"That's the coffee," Katie said. "I'll be right back."

Dawn turned the cold water on in the tub and splashed some on Willow's face. "Willow? Can you hear me? Willow?" She splashed her face again, but still got no reaction.

"I hate to say it, but this is for your own good," she muttered, reaching over to stop up the tub and turning on the cold water.

When Katie limped back into the bathroom with a cup of black coffee, Willow was already lying in two inches of icy water and she hadn't so much as budged.

"Switch it to shower," Dawn said. "Wait, help me up first, please."

Katie put the coffee cup on the sink and helped Dawn get back to her chair just outside of the bathroom. Then she turned the shower on full force.

Willow came to with a yelp as the frigid water hit her face. "Stop! Stop it!" she shrieked.

"No can do," Dawn called. "Keep the water going, Katie."

Willow screeched and sputtered as the water flowed into her mouth and her nose at the same time. "Hey! Stop, I

mean it!" she spluttered, splashing one hand ineffectually in
the bathwater.

"Time for coffee," Dawn said.

Katie reached for the coffee and tried to hand it to
Willow, getting soaked by the shower spray in the process.

"She won't be able to hold it," Dawn said. "Hold the cup
for her and let her sip."

"I don' wan' it." Willow's words were slurred, and her
head lolled to the side as she closed her eyes again.

"Oh, no, you don't," Katie said, water dripping down her
face. She opened Willow's mouth and literally poured some
coffee into her. Most of it dribbled down Willow's chest to
mix in with the bathwater.

"Just keep doing it. Eventually some of it will get into her
system. Hey, Willow!" Dawn yelled. "Did you take any
pills?" She looked at Katie. "You didn't see any pills, did
you?"

"No." Katie forced some more coffee into the protesting
Willow as she spoke. "I feel like this is my fault, Dawn. I
knew she was secretly drinking. I mean, I suspected. And I
didn't say anything about it. I was afraid she'd be mad at
me."

"Willow is her own responsibility, Katie," Dawn said
firmly. "Believe me, I learned that once I had my accident.
Whatever her problem is, she's the one who needs to deal
with it."

Just like I need to deal with Kelly, she thought. *It's not
Kelly's fault if she can go hiking and I can't. If only she
would return my phone calls I could—*

"I can hol' it," Willow said, her voice small and shaky.

"Progress!" Katie cried happily. "Drink the whole cup.
I've got two pots of the stuff."

Willow's teeth were chattering as she sipped the coffee.

"Freezin'," she said, her whole body shaking. "He'p me out?"

She reached for Katie's hands as Katie stood up on trembling legs. She managed to get Willow to the bed, where the girl collapsed. Dawn covered her with all the blankets while Katie got a towel to dry her hair. Then Katie gave Willow more coffee and went to retrieve the girl's robe from the bathroom.

As she returned to the bed she noticed a small piece of paper fall out of the pocket of the robe.

MEET ME IN THE TENTH-FLOOR STAIRWELL TONIGHT FIFTEEN MINUTES AFTER BED CHECK IF YOU KNOW WHAT'S GOOD FOR YOU.

What could that be? Katie wondered. She stuffed the note into her pocket and took Willow her robe.

"I dunno know whah you, you, you . . ." Willow could hardly get the words out, she was so drunk.

"Because we care about you," Dawn said. "I don't know why you did it, Willow, but I can't stay around to find out now. I've got to go get ready for the pageant." She looked at Katie. "Will you be okay?"

"I'm fine," Katie assured her. "You're a lifesaver."

After Dawn left, Katie refilled Willow's coffee cup and handed it to her.

"Uh . . . I'm gonna pee-ook," Willow moaned.

"Can you make it to the bathroom?"

"Mebbe," Willow said. She got out of bed and staggered into the bathroom, where she gagged and threw up into the toilet over and over.

Finally, barely able to walk, she stumbled back into the bedroom and crawled into bed.

"Want some water?" Katie asked. "Or should I order some ginger ale?"

Tears were leaking from Willow's eyes. "I'm so sorry, Katie."

"Why did you do this?" Katie demanded.

For a moment, in her drunken state, Willow wanted to confess everything. Her drinking. And the drunk-driving arrest when she'd hit that little boy. Rehab. And then secretly drinking again but all the time lying to everyone—her friends, her parents—and pretending to be sober.

Allison's scheme to coerce her out of the pageant.

No. I can't confess, Willow thought woozily. *I'm too ashamed. Too ashamed. And right after the pageant, I really am going to stop drinking.*

"I'm nervous, I guess," she lied, "and I only drank a little. This much." She held up two fingers sideways, and Katie knew she was lying.

"Half-full," Willow mumbled. "It wasn't half-full." She took another sip of the black coffee.

"Are you sure?" Katie asked. "Or does it all have something to do with this?" She took the note she'd found out of her pocket and held it up.

Willow took it from her. "That's not any of your affair."

"Fine. Have it your way. I have to get ready for the pageant."

"Katie I . . . I can't—can't tell you," Willow said. "Understand?"

"How can I understand when I don't know what there is to understand?" Katie asked.

Willow was silent.

"Fine, then, be that way." There was bitterness in Katie's voice. "I'm taking a shower. Drink the rest of the coffee, Willow. You're going to need it. You're due onstage in four and a half hours."

CHAPTER 16

Mrs. Crownwell-Stevens was standing at a podium on the left side of the stage in her glittering mauve evening gown as she addressed the audience of three hundred people.

"Ladies and gentlemen, judges, honored guests, please welcome the host and hostess of the Miss Southern Teen Spirit Pageant, Leena Sharpe and Brendan Hamway!"

Leena Sharpe, a popular anchorwoman from one of the local TV stations, and Brendan Hamway, an up-and-coming country singer, walked onto the stage to enthusiastic applause.

"I am so excited to be here, Brendan, aren't you?" Leena asked.

"I sure am, Leena. Imagine me onstage with thirty gorgeous girls!"

"Better watch it, Brendan," Leena joked. "Not only are these girls just seventeen years old, but they're smart, talented, and young leaders in their communities. Besides, I hear Miss Teen Spirit North Carolina has a black belt in karate!"

The audience chuckled appreciatively.

"Seriously, ladies and gentlemen," Brendan said, "we truly are proud to be your host and hostess for the first regional competition of the very first Miss Teen Spirit Pageant. Following this pageant, there will be regional pageants in the Midwest, North, and West. Each pageant will send six lucky girls to the national finals in Orlando, Florida, held later in the year. And there, one very lucky girl will be crowned Miss Teen Spirit."

Leena went on to list all the things Miss Teen Spirit would win, as well as the prizes for the six winners of the regional pageants.

Backstage, the girls were a bundle of nerves. In just a moment they would all parade out onto the stage for the opening number of the pageant. Each girl was dressed in a costume that she felt reflected her home state or the organization she was representing. Each girl would walk to the center microphone and announce her name and her title.

"Willow, how are you doing?" Katie asked. She took her roommate's hands in hers. They were ice-cold.

"Shakes," Willow admitted. "But I'm here. How about you?"

"I can actually put a little weight on my ankle," Katie said, demonstrating. "I still have to go out there with my crutches, though."

"Good luck, Katie. You deserve it."

Katie smiled back at her friend.

"And now, please welcome our thirty wonderful girls!" she heard Leena Sharpe saying from the stage.

"Go!" Jimmy Delancy ordered as the orchestra began to play the music for the opening parade. The girls smiled and the parade began. In alphabetical order, according to the title they held, each girl walked to the microphone to introduce herself.

First was Gillian Chapell, a girl who had mostly kept to herself. She was dressed in a tiny polka-dot, off-the-shoulder top and tiny shorts, like Daisy Mae from Li'l Abner. "Hey, y'all!" she cried, winking at the audience. "I'm Gillian Chapell, Miss Teen Spirit Alabama!"

All the girls paraded across the stage, and one by one, they approached the microphone. Beth Kaplan wore a costume that had turned her into a giant orange tree, to represent Florida. Willow, although shaky, looked beautiful in a French cancan outfit to represent the French Quarter of New Orleans as Miss Teen Spirit Louisiana. Scarlett-Caress made a great impression dressed as Scarlett O'Hara for Miss Teen Spirit of the South.

Finally, it was Dawn's turn. To represent Mississippi, she was dressed as a riverboat gambler, and she looked darling. But as she wheeled herself toward the microphone she realized that neither she, nor anyone else, had thought about the fact that the microphone would be much too high for her to reach.

Jimmy rushed out onstage to lower the mike for her, but Dawn waved him off. "No need, I've got great lungs!" she yelled. She turned to the audience and threw her voice to the very back of the room. "Hi, I'm the girl with the loud voice, Dawn Faison, Miss Teen Spirit Mississippi!"

The audience applauded for her as she wheeled herself back into the parade line.

The next big audience pleaser was Shyanne, Miss Teen Spirit Southern Rodeo Queen, who came out in suede, fringed riding chaps, riding on a stick pony. Wanda Sue wowed the crowd as Miss Teen Spirit Southern Beauty. She was covered from just above her breasts to just below her thighs in flowers that were indigenous to the South.

Michelle Evans was fantastic in a red-white-and-blue-fringed leotard. She did flips all the way to the microphone and then announced herself as Miss Teen Spirit Southern Fitness.

Allison appeared outfitted as a soldier, her costume half-Confederate and half-Union. She carried an American flag. "I'm Allison Gaylord, proud to be part of this great nation, united under God above, Miss Teen Spirit Southern Star!" she said proudly into the microphone.

Then it was Katie's turn. Jane had helped her sew her Thomas Jefferson costume. In her hand, she carried a scroll representing the Declaration of Independence as she limped up to the microphone on her crutches and announced, "Hi, I'm Katie Laramie, injured in the line of duty. From the land of Thomas Jefferson, I'm Miss Teen Spirit Virginia."

Finally, the parade was over. As Dean was performing a medley of Southern songs onstage, the girls were next door changing into their matching blue-and-white leotards under a short, red cheerleading skirt, their costume for the fitness parade and dance number.

If I can get through this I can get through anything, Dawn thought as she struggled to get into her leotard.

"Just remember, honey lamb," Scarlett-Caress told her as they waited to go back onstage for the dance number. "You are worth ten girls like The Virus. And probably five girls like me."

"I know, I know, you admire me to death," Dawn said nervously.

Scarlett-Caress's face broke into a grin. "Now, how did you know?"

The girls went through the dance number. Dawn spun around in her wheelchair, center stage. Through it all she had a big smile plastered on her face. Just a few days earlier

Jimmy had decided that each girl would have a solo moment during the number, to show off her physical fitness.

According to Jimmy's choreography, when it was Dawn's turn, she was supposed to pop a wheelie with her wheelchair, then smile and shrug in a way that would look both cute and helpless.

But when her turn came, that's not what she did. Instead she took three tennis balls that she'd put in her lap and expertly juggled them, as her wheelchair tennis coach had taught her one rainy day last year. She finished by spinning her wheelchair around and catching the last ball behind her back.

It had all been Scarlett-Caress's idea.

And somehow, when the number ended and Dawn was center stage holding that huge American flag while all the other girls knelt around her, she didn't feel quite so bad.

As the girls hurried next door to change into their evening gowns, Leena and Brendan introduced the executives from *Teen Spirit* magazine, and then they introduced all the judges. Following that, the orchestra played a medley of famous songs about Tennessee to give the girls more time.

The scene next door was one of utter chaos. Though many assistants were on hand to help the girls change and the walls were lined with mirrored dressing tables, it was still a frantic, hysterical zoo.

"My bra strap broke!" Wanda Sue yelled in a panic.

"Wear your backup bra!" a harried assistant screamed as she ran by with a pair of panty hose.

"I can't. It'll show under my gown! I need a strapless!"

"I just got powder on my gown!" Donna Juarez yelped. "How do you get powder off velvet?"

Katie had finished changing into her pale blue gown. It had puff sleeves, a tulle skirt, and a demure sweetheart neckline. She and Jane had found it on sale at a wedding-and-bridal-party outlet store. She looked over at Wanda Sue, who had poured herself into a slinky midnight-blue number, clearly with no bra underneath.

Next to her I look like I'm about ten years old, Katie thought anxiously. She tried to keep in mind that the pageant handbook had suggested that the girls look wholesome and sweet, as opposed to sexy, in their gowns.

Willow stood in front of one of the mirrors, pinning her hair up with shaking fingers.

"Need help?" Katie offered.

"I don't deserve it," Willow said.

Wordlessly, Katie took the hairpins from Willow and helped pin up the back of her hair.

Willow's dress was, of course, both stunning and simple. Sleeveless white chiffon held up with a simple band of material that wrapped around her long, elegant neck; the lightweight fabric fell from tucks across the bodice, drifting elegantly around her body.

She looked pale, but beautiful.

Soon the girls were offstage waiting as Dean finished singing his medley.

It's not the dress, Katie reminded herself as she compared her dress with Allison's obviously expensive mint-green off-the-shoulder gown. *It's the girl* in *the dress.*

Allison walked over to Willow. "You have more guts than brains," she whispered in Willow's ear.

Willow didn't even look at her.

"You're dead, Willow," Allison said. Then she walked back to her place in line.

After the applause for Dean, Leena and Brendan reintroduced the judges to the audience.

Then it was time for the girls to go on again.

Each girl was escorted onto the stage by a uniformed young man from a nearby prep school while the orchestra played "The Tennessee Waltz." Dawn held her head high as she wheeled herself out next to her escort. Katie limped as gracefully as she could on her crutches. Wanda Sue almost tripped over the bottom of her gown.

Now it was time for the judges to choose the twelve semifinalists. Only those twelve girls would give mini-versions of their platform speeches, as well as perform their talent.

And from those twelve girls would come the final six, the lucky contestants who would each win five thousand dollars and go on to compete in the national pageant.

To give the judges time to complete their ballots, Brendan Hamway sang his current hit song. Then the national clogging champions came onstage and did a rousing dance number to "Turkey in the Straw."

Finally, it was time to announce the twelve semifinalists. All the girls were onstage, smiles plastered on their faces.

"Well, Brendan, I've got the judges' decisions for the semifinalists," Leena said. "Are you ready?"

"Sure am, Leena. But I'd just like to say that all these girls are fantastic. I'll tell you what; I'm sure glad I don't have to pick out twelve of 'em!"

"If your name is called as a semifinalist, please step forward," Leena said. "The names will be called in no particular order. Please let's hold our applause until all the names are called."

A moment of hushed silence.

"The semifinalists for the Miss Southern Teen Spirit Pageant are: Michelle Evans, Allison Gaylord, Carly Mitchell, Willow Rose Harrison, Belinda Sweete, Wanda Sue Burnett,

Shyanne Derringer, Dawn Faison, Becky Haas, Anita Lynn Jamison, Katie Laramie, and Scarlett-Caress Latham!"

The audience applauded loudly as eleven girls stepped, and one girl wheeled, forward.

"Well, girls, congratulations," Brendan said. "And best of luck in the rest of the pageant."

All the girls rushed backstage. The twelve semifinalists hurried to change into their talent outfits. The other girls, who knew they had been eliminated, also knew to stay out of their way.

"Dang, Beth got eliminated," Shyanne said to Katie as she quickly changed into her star-spangled rodeo outfit.

"I know," Katie replied as she pulled on her pink leotard. "I can't understand it. She's so smart and talented."

"I can," Scarlett-Caress interjected, brushing her hair and fixing her lipstick. "Beth is a sweetheart, but she doesn't have that beauty-queen sparkle. I told you, it's charisma."

Willow reached for a glass of water, her hands shaking. As time went by she was feeling worse instead of better. And every time Allison looked at her, she wanted to run away.

From across the room, Allison was looking over at Willow now. She held up a piece of paper and dangled it so that Allison could see.

It's my arrest record, Willow thought, panicking. She felt as if she were going to throw up.

Willow was on first for the talent competition. Somehow she made it through her song, but she knew she hadn't been nearly as good as she could have been. Her concentration was shot. Her voice even cracked once, and her legs where shaking under her full skirt.

"Remember, you drunk, you're finished," Allison hissed in her ear when Willow came off stage. Willow pretended she hadn't heard.

But how much longer could she pretend?

Everyone else's talent went just about the same as it had the other night, with the exception of Michelle and Allison, who were both even more dazzling.

This time Katie didn't have Bryan White as a volunteer for her card tricks, but Brendan Hamway offered to help her, and she was able to pull off almost the same act with him.

The mini-versions of the platform speeches went by quickly. And finally, it was time for one of the hosts for the evening to ask each of the twelve semifinalists a question, which they would have to answer spontaneously. It could be about current events, their personal convictions on an issue of the day, or just about anything.

Brendan held a microphone and walked over to the line of girls, all of whom had changed back into their evening gowns. One by one, each girl answered a question. Allison, Carly, Belinda, Becky, Anita, Michelle, Shyanne, and Scarlett-Caress answered their questions smoothly. Dawn gave a standout answer to her question about mainstreaming kids with physical disabilities. Wanda Sue stumbled a little over answering a question about mandatory curfews for teens.

The last two girls in line were Katie and Willow.

"Well, Katie, you're next to last," Brendan said. "I bet you wish you had those giant playing cards now!"

"I really do," Katie agreed with a grin.

"Here's your question. "In this day and age, do you believe that poverty holds a teen back from following her dreams?"

"Yes," Katie replied with no hesitation, and she heard a murmur of surprise from the audience. "And no," she added. "We live in a wonderful country, with wonderful opportunities, but we don't yet live in a country where poor kids have the resources to fully compete with privileged kids. However, I have learned through my own experience that if one person really believes in you, you're not poor at all. With that person's love and support, and a lot of hard work, your dreams can still come true."

The audience applauded like crazy.

Katie knew that somewhere out in the audience, Jane was one of those people clapping.

That was for you, Jane, she thought. *No matter what happens, I hope I did you proud.*

"Willow Rose Harrison, what a great name," Brendan said, moving on to Willow.

Katie looked over at her roommate. Willow's face was almost as white as her gown. "Thank you," Willow said softly.

"Willow, there's a big problem on our roads today with teens drinking and driving. What do you think we can do as a society to help with this problem?"

The first thought that flew into Willow's mind was: *Allison told him about me!*

Then she thought, *But no, that couldn't be true. It was just a terrible coincidence. Wasn't it?*

"Willow, your answer?" Brendan asked.

Cold sweat popped out on Willow's forehead. Down the line, Allison caught her eye. "I think that . . ." Her voice trailed off.

"I'm afraid I have to ask for your answer," Brendan said.

"I . . . it's bad to drink and drive," Willow said. "It's . . . very bad."

The other girls onstage tried not to look as stunned as they felt. Willow was the best of all of them. And she had just failed, right before their eyes.

The girls rushed offstage as Dean sang another number, which he dedicated to the girls who had been eliminated.

"Willow?" Katie asked, grabbing her friend's arm. "Are you okay?"

"I'm . . ." Willow sagged against Katie.

"What can I get you?"

"Water," Willow whispered.

An assistant ran off to locate a glass of water. Someone else quickly provided a chair. Willow sank into it, silent tears running down her cheeks.

From a few feet away, Allison Gaylord was smiling.

"And now, ladies and gentlemen, the moment you've all been waiting for," Brendan said. "It's time to announce the six winners of the Miss Southern Teen Spirit Pageant. These six girls will go on to the National Teen Spirit Pageant in Orlando, which will be televised internationally by a special syndicated broadcast."

Leena handed the envelope to Brendan. "Brendan, will you do the honors?"

"I have to tell you, I'm as nervous as you girls are," Brendan said.

The twelve girls stood in line, holding hands.

"If I call your name, please step forward," Brendan said. "The names that I call will be our six winners, in no particular order. When y'all compete in the national pageant, they tell me everyone's score will start back at zero. Well, here we go!"

Brendan read the card in his hands. "Our six winners are: Scarlett-Caress Latham, Miss Pride of the South! Michelle Evans, Miss Southern Fitness! Wanda Sue Burnett, Miss Southern Beauty!"

He took a breath as Scarlett, Michelle, and Wanda Sue hugged each other.

"There are still three more names," Brendan said. Katie held Dawn's hand on one side, and Willow's on the other.

Please let all three of us get it, she prayed. *Please.*

"Our fourth winner is Dawn Faison, Miss Mississippi!"

"Oh my God," Dawn breathed as the audience broke into overwhelming applause.

"Go," Katie told her, her eyes shining with happiness for her friend.

Dawn wheeled herself into the line of winners.

"Well, Leena, there's just two names left," Brendan said.

Katie looked at Willow. Surely Willow had so many points before the last part of the competition that she would be one of the final two girls chosen. And there was Shyanne, who was so dazzling in her talent. And The Virus, of course.

Card tricks with a huge deck of cards was not going to get a girl like me to the nationals, Katie thought. *I was fooling myself all the time.*

"The fifth winner is . . . Katie Laramie, Miss Virginia!"

Katie's hands flew to her mouth. Had he really and truly called her name? Had she really beat Willow and all the others? She looked back at her friend, who, hiding her own disappointment, smiled and applauded.

It really *was* true. From somewhere in the audience, Katie could swear she heard Jane's voice screaming over the other applause as she stepped forward, head held high, to join the winners.

"Okay, one more!" Brendan said. "Let's do it! Your final girl from the South going onto Orlando is . . ."

Let it be Willow, please let it be Willow, Katie prayed, though she knew that the other girl's chances weren't all that good. *Or let it be Shyanne. She's fun. Or Becky, who's so smart, just don't let it be—*

"Miss Allison Gaylord, Miss Teen Southern Star!"

Allison jumped up and punched the air with her fist as Katie's heart sank. Then, The Virus shot a snide look at Willow as she strutted forward and took her place in the line of winners, right next to Katie.

"Congrats, Katie thighs," she hissed, her whisper as nasty as her smile was radiant. "I'll see you in Orlando."

CHAPTER

17

ackstage, pandemonium reigned as friends and family embraced the girls. Katie found Willow by herself in a corner.

"Willow?"

"Congratulations, Katie," Willow said. "You deserved it."

"I just feel so badly—"

"Don't," Willow told her. "I blew it. It's my own fault."

Katie put her hand on Willow's arm. "Do you think . . . I mean, if you have a problem, it's nothing to be ashamed of. You could get some help."

"Maybe I will," Willow said gently.

"Oh, Willow, I'm just *sick* that you didn't make the finals!" Allison said, rushing over to them. "Better luck next time!" She ran off to find her family and friends.

"I detest her," Katie said.

"Me, too," Willow agreed. "But in her own sick way, she did me a favor."

Katie had a feeling this had something to do with that note she had found. "What did she do?"

"I'll tell you sometime, I promise," Willow said. "After all, we're still bestest friends, aren't we?"

"Absolutely," Katie said, and she hugged Willow hard.

Dawn wheeled herself over to Scarlett-Caress, who was talking with two older people that Dawn guessed were her parents. When Scarlett saw her, she tapped Dawn on the shoulder.

"Oh, Mom and Dad, I want you to meet my roommate, Dawn Faison," she said. "Isn't she just the most inspirational thing ever?"

"Why, yes," her mother agreed, "bless your heart!" She looked and sounded just like an older version of Scarlett-Caress. "Honey-ums, it's just too crowded back here. We'll meet you out in the lobby after you change."

Scarlett-Caress turned to Dawn. "So, roomie, you won!"

"So did you."

"Yes, but I was *supposed* to win," Scarlett-Caress said.

"And you never thought I'd make it past the semifinals, even with all your help."

"That's true," Scarlett-Caress admitted. "I guess I'm a better teacher than I realized."

Dawn laughed. "You had a lot to work with."

"I did, didn't I? See you at the nationals, roomie. And don't expect so many free tips next time," she added, grinning at Dawn. "After all, now you're competition!"

"Dawn?"

Dawn wheeled herself around.

"Kelly! Oh gosh, I had no idea you were here!"

"Your parents brought me," Kelly said, hugging Dawn. "They're waiting outside. Dawn, I was so proud of you."

"Why didn't you return any of my phone calls?" Dawn asked. "I was so worried—"

"I was kind of busy," Kelly said, her voice low.

"Too busy to even call me?"

"I . . . I had to go to the doctor. I . . . got kind of sick on the hiking trip. And I've been so tired lately, and I get all these bruises."

"What is it?" Dawn asked, afraid to hear the answer.

"I'm getting the test results tomorrow," Kelly said.

"Nothing, maybe," Dawn said hopefully. She reached for Kelly's hand.

Kelly's lips trembled. "Maybe. But I think it's something. Something bad. Like . . . like maybe leukemia."

"No, Kelly. It can't be!"

Kelly put a smile on her face and pulled her hand away from Dawn's. "Hey, let's not talk about it now. This is your day!"

"But, Kel—"

"I'm sure you're right. It's nothing. I shouldn't have even bothered you with it. Let's go see your folks. They're so excited for you they're about to pass out from happiness. Today, we celebrate!"

Allison put her makeup into her toiletries case and slipped the plastic back over her evening gown. No one from her family had come to see her in the pageant; not her mother, not her father, and not her identical twin, Megan, who lived with their father in Chicago. Well, she hadn't expected them to, really. They didn't like her any better than she liked them.

Besides, she was sick of hearing about how good and sweet and nice and smart and wonderful Megan was. Once

Allison won Miss Teen Spirit, her family and everyone else would be singing a new tune.

She *would* win, too. Everything was going her way. Look what had happened to Gigi—although that had just been Allison's good luck. She had certainly outsmarted that twit, Willow-the-Perfect. She felt certain she could outsmart any other girl, too.

The wheels were already turning in her head. She had to find a way to get to all three of the other regional pageants without being seen, since it was strictly against the stupid rules for her to attend.

I will find a way, though, Allison thought as she zipped up her makeup case. *No one is as determined as I am. I do whatever I have to do to win. I'll cheat and steal and lie and kill—*

Kill? Would I really? she wondered.

And then she smiled to herself.

Because she already knew the answer.

"Katie Laramie, I'm so proud of you I could bust," came Jane's sweet voice from behind her.

"Oh, Jane!" Katie cried. Jane held out her arms and she hobbled into them.

"What did you do to yourself?" Jane asked through her happy tears.

"I sprained my ankle practicing on the trampoline," Katie explained.

"Well, your card tricks were a delight," Jane said.

Katie's eyes shown with happiness. "Jane, five thousand dollars! I just won five thousand dollars! I can't believe it!"

"I can," Jane said, hugging Katie again. "As soon as we get home, we'll start working toward the nationals."

"Do you really, truly think I have a chance?" Katie asked.

"Don't you?" Jane asked.

"I don't know . . . I never thought I'd get this far," Katie admitted.

"Katie Laramie, you can go as far as you can dream," Jane said. "Because you're one of the rare ones."

"Rare ones?" Katie echoed.

Jane nodded. "You're willing to do the hard work to make your dreams come true. I want you to know that I was deeply touched by what you said onstage, about one person believing in you."

"I'd never be here without you, Jane."

"And I'd never be here without you, Katie," Jane said, laughing.

"Hey, Miss Back Bay," a teasing male voice said. "Congratulations."

Katie smiled at Dean. "Thanks. I want you to meet my friend Jane Emery," she said. "Jane, this is Dean Paisley."

"Nice to meet you." Jane smiled warmly. "You're very talented."

"Thanks," Dean said. "Wasn't Katie great?"

"Dean taught me the card tricks, Jane."

"Hey, do you mind if I tear Katie away for just a minute?" Dean asked Jane.

"Go ahead," Jane said. "How about if I wait for you next door and help you carry your stuff up to your room?"

Dean led Katie through the backstage crowd.

"Hey, slow down, I'm only semimobile!" Katie protested.

Dean didn't respond. Instead he led her out a back door. The hallway was empty. Without saying a word, he picked her up in his arms and carried her down the hall and into a small, empty conference room.

"Are we having a meeting?" Katie asked as Dean put her down.

"A meeting of two," he answered. He moved close to her and touched her cheek. "You won, Katie."

"You helped me win."

"Unless my 'attitude problem' gets in the way again, this means I'll see you at the nationals."

"That will be nice," Katie whispered.

"But, Katie, I need to see you again sooner than that," Dean murmured. "I'm off for the next week before the next pageant starts. And I'd really like to visit Back Bay, Virginia, if you wouldn't mind showing me around."

"I could do that," Katie said, her heart soaring.

"Good." He put his arms around her waist. "And one last thing."

"What's that?"

Dean's voice was low. "There's something I have to tell you."

"What?"

"This," Dean told her. Then he took her into his arms and gave her the sweetest kiss in the history of kisses. "Katie Laramie," he said, when he finally stopped kissing her, "this is only the beginning. You are going to do incredible things with your life."

As Katie melted into his kiss again, for the first time she really believed, with all her heart, that it was true.